W9-AHB-185

Ex-Library: Friends of
Lake County Public Library

THE
CREEPING
SHADOWS

Ex-Libris
Lake County

THE CREEPING SHADOWS

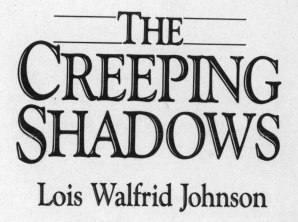

Lois Walfrid Johnson

BETHANY HOUSE PUBLISHERS
MINNEAPOLIS, MINNESOTA 55438

3 3113 01680 6152

Except for Rev. Augustus Nelson and Big Gust Anderson, village marshall Grantsburg, Wisconsin, in the early 1900s, the characters in this book are fictitious. Any resemblance to persons living or dead is coincidental.

Copyright © 1990
Lois Walfrid Johnson
All Rights Reserved

Published by Bethany House Publishers
A Ministry of Bethany Fellowship, Inc.
6820 Auto Club Road, Minneapolis, Minnesota 55438

Printed in the United States of America

Library of Congress Cataloging-in-Publication Data

Johnson, Lois Walfrid.
    The creeping shadows / Lois Walfrid Johnson.
      p.   cm. — (The Adventures of the northwoods ; bk. 3)
    Summary: Kate plans a birthday party for her stepbrother Anders and gets involved in the mysterious disappearance of items from the Erickson household.

    [1. Swedish Americans—Fiction. 2. Stepfamilies—Fiction.
3. Mystery and detective stories. 4. Christian life—Fiction.]
I. Title. II. Series: Johnson, Lois Walfrid. Adventures of the northwoods ;
3.
PZ7.J63255Cr 1990
[Fic]—dc20
ISBN 1–55661–102–1

90–49143
CIP
AC

To Walter and Ella Johnson,

friends I can count on,

with thanks

for remembering the way it was.

LOIS WALFRID JOHNSON is the bestselling author of more than twenty books. These include *You're Worth More Than You Think!* and other Gold Medallion winners in the LET'S-TALK-ABOUT-IT STORIES FOR KIDS series about making choices. Novels in the ADVENTURES OF THE NORTHWOODS series have received awards from Excellence in Media, the Wisconsin State Historical Society, and the Council for Wisconsin Writers.

Lois has a great interest in historical mystery novels, as you may be able to tell! She and her husband, Roy, are the parents of a blended family and live in rural Wisconsin.

Contents

1. Trouble Ahead 9
2. Maybelle Pendleton 15
3. Stretch! 21
4. The Unwanted Visitor 29
5. Josie's Secret 35
6. Howls in the Night 43
7. The Search 51
8. City Girl Farmer 55
9. Wildfire! 63
10. Race Against Time 67
11. Kate's Choice 73
12. Out of the Darkness 81
13. Papa's Strange Letter 85
14. The Moving Shadow 91
15. Discovery! 99
16. The Loan Shark Returns 105
17. Frightening News 113
18. Growing Threats ∴ 119
19. The Shadows Lengthen 127
20. Lutfisk Meets Calico 133
21. Footsteps Through the Snow 139
22. The Dangerous Chase 147
23. Northern Lights 153
Acknowledgments 159

Adventures
of the Northwoods

1. *The Disappearing Stranger*

2. *The Hidden Message*

3. *The Creeping Shadows*

4. *The Vanishing Footprints*

5. *Trouble at Wild River*

6. *The Mysterious Hideaway*

7. *Grandpa's Stolen Treasure*

8. *The Runaway Clown*

1

Trouble Ahead

A gust of wind swooped around the corner, caught the barn door, and flung it back on its hinges. As the door banged against the wall, Katherine O'Connell pushed aside the black hair escaping her braid. In the December air her cheeks were red with cold.

A troubled look darkened Kate's deep blue eyes. *Today Papa Nordstrom returns to logging camp*, she thought. *What if something goes wrong when he's gone?* Already there'd been mysterious happenings around Windy Hill Farm.

Pulling off her mittens, Kate reached through the high rail fence to stroke the star on Wildfire's forehead. The mare's smooth coat shone in the early morning sunlight. She moved closer, nuzzling Kate's neck.

Kate laughed. "If you could talk, would you have secrets to tell?"

The mare tossed her head as though saying yes, and Kate laughed again. Picking up a bucket, Kate held it out.

Black and sleek, long-legged with four white socks, Wildfire dipped her head into the oats. But a minute later she lifted her ears and stepped back.

"You don't want oats?" Kate felt puzzled. "What's wrong?"

Still reaching through the fence, she held the bucket higher.

Instead of coming forward, Wildfire edged farther back. Raising her head, the mare turned her ears to listen. The next moment she snorted and struck the ground with her front hoof.

Kate dropped the bucket and jumped away from the fence. "Wildfire, what's wrong?"

Again the mare snorted and struck the ground several times. Her eyes rolled.

Kate's heart thudded. In the months she'd known Wildfire, the mare had never acted like this.

An instant later a howl broke the early morning stillness. Starting low, it rose, dropped, then rose again. In the cold air the sound lingered in the trees.

Kate shivered. A wolf. Across the field, somewhere in the woods. How far away?

Just then Kate heard a shout. She swung around, glad for human company. Her new brother Anders stood on the path leading to the house.

Though twelve years old like Kate, Anders was tall for his age. His wide shoulders stretched the seams of his jacket and blond hair fell over his forehead. Setting his crutches ahead of him, he swung forward.

A few days ago Anders had sprained his ankle. Yet so far crutches hadn't kept him from anything he wanted to do.

Stopping on the snow-covered path, he called again, "Kate! Papa wants you!"

Nine months before, in March 1906, Kate's widowed mother had married Anders' father, Carl Nordstrom. Mama and Kate had moved to Windy Hill Farm in northwest Wisconsin.

As Kate ran to meet Anders, he looked her in the face. "What's the matter? You're scared."

"A wolf, Anders." Kate's voice trembled. "I heard a wolf."

"Don't worry," he said. "It won't hurt you."

Kate didn't believe him. "Did you hear Wildfire whinny?"

"Yup." Anders didn't seem to care. "She'll be your first warning that anything's around. But forget it now. Papa has to leave."

As Kate hurried into the farmhouse, the warmth of the wood cookstove reached out. Yet the kitchen was quiet—too quiet. To

Kate it seemed colder than if she were feeling the December wind.

On Christmas Eve, Papa Nordstrom had returned from the logging camp where he'd worked since November. Only yesterday the family celebrated Christmas together. Was it already time to say goodbye?

A knot of dread tightened Kate's stomach as she joined the family at the table: her new sister, blond five-year-old Tina; her new brother, nine-year-old Lars; Anders; Mama; and Papa Nordstrom.

Mama had trimmed Papa's brown hair, mustache, and beard. Yet his chapped face still showed the bite of walking home in the winter wind. His eyes looked soft, as though he already felt the separation from his family.

"Sven will be here soon," Papa told them, his voice heavy.

Sven would drive into Grantsburg, giving Papa a ride to the train. Kate had known that since yesterday, but now the separation seemed real. And Kate felt something more. An uneasiness swept through her like the wind sighing in a pine tree.

"Do you really have to go?" Her question burst out, though she knew it would do no good to ask.

"We need seed money for spring planting," Papa reminded her.

"But what will we do without you?" The question hung in the air as Kate thought of all the things that could go wrong on a Wisconsin farm. When Papa left in November, she'd asked the same question. She had found out.

Strange things had taken place. She and Anders and their friend Erik had needed to solve a mystery. What might happen now, with Papa gone again, and the long, dark days of January just ahead?

"Kate," Mama said softly, as though warning her not to speak about something that couldn't be changed.

But instead Kate asked, "You came all that way to be here just one day?"

Papa nodded, and for an instant Kate wondered if his eyes were wet.

"I had to know how all of you are," he said, looking around

the table. Reaching out a hand, he placed it on top of Mama's.

"We needed Christmas together," she added. Tall for a woman, with golden blond hair, Mama was expecting a baby in the spring. Under her large apron her usually slim waist was growing.

"Sorry I'll miss your birthday, Anders," said Papa.

Mine, too, thought Kate, but didn't say it aloud. There was something she wanted to know. She remembered the construction accident that killed her Irish father, Daddy O'Connell. "Is it dangerous, working at the logging camp?"

Papa glanced quickly toward Mama, then back at Kate. "Sometimes," he said softly. "But it might also be hard for all of you here without me. We must pray every day for each other. Soon I'll be home again."

Still holding Mama's hand, Papa bowed his head and prayed in Swedish. As she heard their names, Kate guessed he was praying for each member of the family. Yet she couldn't understand Papa's words. Mama had come from Sweden, but Daddy O'Connell had been Irish. They had always spoken English in their home.

A moment later Papa Nordstrom stopped and cleared his throat. He switched into English, as though recalling Kate didn't know what he said. "Heavenly Father," he prayed, his voice deep. "When Kate needs to remember, remind her of thy care for her."

Surprised at Papa's prayer, Kate swallowed. Quickly she brushed away the tear that slid down her cheek.

Then Papa said, "Ah-men."

Kate glanced up to see Anders watching her. But instead of his usual teasing, he looked away.

When sleigh bells jingled in the farmyard, Papa slowly stood up, as though not wanting the time to end. He pulled on his heavy coat and boots, then hugged all of them.

Swinging forward on crutches, Anders followed Papa into the yard. Kate trailed behind, stopping just outside the door.

As he reached the sleigh, Papa looked Anders square in the eyes. "It's been a long time since Mama lived on a farm in winter," he said. "And Kate never has."

Shivering in the cold, Kate strained to hear, but the wind caught his next words and took them away. Papa reached out his hand, resting it on Anders' shoulder. He spoke again, but Kate still could not hear.

The back of Anders' blond head moved as though he were nodding.

Papa brushed a mittened hand across his eyes. *Is he crying?* Kate wondered. At this distance she couldn't be sure. Then Papa's words came clear in the December air. "Take care of Mama and Kate, won't you? And Tina and Lars."

Anders straightened his broad shoulders and stood taller. His father's strong arms wrapped around him. Then Papa climbed onto the sleigh.

Sven flicked the reins, and the horses stepped out. When Papa turned back and waved at Anders, he looked toward the house. Seeing Kate, he waved again.

As the sleigh passed beyond the barn and out of sight, Kate's eyes blurred with tears.

2

Maybelle Pendleton

$\mathcal{K}$ate shivered and hurried back into the kitchen. More than once she'd plunged headlong into adventure, sometimes with surprising results. But now Kate watched quietly as her mother turned away from the window. In the silence Mama sniffled once and hurried over to the cookstove.

As Anders dropped into a chair, Mama lifted a stove lid. Pushing in a corncob, she pulled the teakettle over the firebox. But even then she kept her back toward the children.

"Erik's coming soon," Anders said after a time. Erik was Anders' best friend.

Kate barely heard. She was looking at Mama.

"He'll be here *soon*," Anders prodded Kate, even though he, too, watched Mama. "You better get ready."

Her back still turned to them, Mama took the corner of her apron and wiped one eye, then the other. Taking a deep breath, she straightened her shoulders.

When Mama turned their way, her face showed no tears. But her blue eyes held a shadow—a shadow Kate hadn't seen since the time following Daddy O'Connell's death.

Mama cleared her throat. "I'm glad you want to help out, collecting meat for Swensons." Her voice sounded almost normal. "They have a hard time making their money go far enough. I hope they don't lose their farm."

"Josie's got a big family," Anders said gruffly. "Eight brothers and sisters. Nine children is a lot to feed."

"Yah," said Mama. "But I think it's more than that. Mrs. Swenson often seems worried. And she's not the worrying kind."

Josie Swenson was a special friend to both Kate and Anders. Her father had fattened an animal for two years to have meat for this winter. In November the steer was stolen.

Two days before, on the afternoon of Christmas Eve, Kate, Anders, and Erik had solved the mystery of that theft. But they also learned the steer was gone for good.

Reaching for his crutches, Anders stood up. "I'd better get going. Every family I asked promised to help out."

He made it sound as if it weren't important, but Kate saw his eyes. It had been Anders' idea to collect meat and other food from any neighbor who wanted to give. On Christmas Day he'd quietly gone to each of the families in their church.

Kate hurried to put on warmer clothes. By the time Erik drove up with the big Lundgren horses, she was ready.

As Kate went outside, Erik jumped down from the sleigh. "Mornin', Kate," he said, solemn as a judge. A warm cap covered most of his wavy brown hair.

"Mornin', Erik," she answered in the same tone of voice.

It had become a joke between them, a joke started the day Erik put the end of her long braid into his inkwell at Spirit Lake School. Now his eyes danced as he grinned down at her. "Great day for a run!"

Kate agreed. For a moment she forgot that Papa had gone back to the logging camp. Feeling the sunlight warm upon her face, she laughed just thinking about the ride across new snow. It was always fun being with Erik.

Lifting the bundle over the high board sides of the sleigh, Kate and Erik loaded the meat Mama had put aside for Swensons. Kate wrapped burlap around bricks she'd warmed, then climbed up to sit next to Erik. Placing the bricks near her feet, she pulled a heavy robe over her lap and tucked it under her legs. In the cold wind she'd be glad for the warmth.

Throwing his crutches into the back, Anders pulled himself up next to Kate. Erik clucked the horses, and they started down the long track to the main road.

The snow sparkled in the sunlight, and tall trees cast blue-gray shadows. Sleigh bells jingled, bright and clear in the crisp December air.

Kate drew a deep breath. On a morning like this, it was easy to believe that northwest Wisconsin was a good place to live. In Minneapolis, Sarah Livingston and Michael Reilly had been her best friends. Here Kate had learned to depend on Anders, Josie Swenson, and Erik Lundgren. Best of all, Kate had started to feel she belonged.

Yet now when Mama couldn't hear, Kate had a question for Anders. "Will Papa be all right?"

Anders looked as though he were planning a smart remark. Then his eyes turned serious, and Kate remembered he never lied to her.

"I hope so," he told her, his voice less certain than usual. "I sure hope so."

Erik flicked the reins, and the horses picked up speed. "Good idea you had," he told Anders. "About bringing food, I mean."

"*Great* idea!" Anders answered with his lopsided grin. He winked at Kate.

Kate pretended she didn't notice, but Anders wouldn't let her get by with it.

"You like my ideas, don't you, Kate?"

"Yah, sure, big brother."

"Like the time I made the bell not work."

Kate smiled, remembering what he'd done to the bell at Spirit Lake School. That plan had been a good one.

"And your first day of school. Remember, little sister?"

Kate frowned. "Just because I'm short for my age, I'm *not* your little sister!"

"Remember how I helped you cross the log over the creek?"

"Help, all right!" Kate laughed. "You were the biggest help I've ever seen!"

Anders paid no attention. "And remember the time I drove Wildfire too fast?"

"The time!" Kate exclaimed. "The *times*, you mean!" She felt uneasy, wondering what Anders would do next. Hoping to get his mind off trying something else, Kate changed the subject. "We'll get to see Josie's new kitten."

Erik grinned. "Her vanishing kitten, you mean. Maybe you can solve that mystery too." Every now and then Swensons couldn't find Calico, even though Josie never let the kitten outside.

All morning long Erik drove from one farm to the next, collecting food. It was midafternoon when he and Kate and Anders reached the other side of Spirit Lake School. Erik turned the horses off the road into yet another farmyard.

"Who lives here?" Kate asked.

"Maybelle," Anders said, as if he were making a big introduction. "Maybelle Pendleton."

"Pendleton?" Kate asked. "She can't be a Swede."

Anders grinned at Erik. "Only half Swede. The half that's right pretty."

Erik's neck flushed red, but he kept his eyes straight ahead.

Kate looked from one to the other. There was something here she didn't understand. "Who's Maybelle Pendleton? How come I've never heard of her before?"

"She and her folks just came home," Anders said. "Moved away for a while, but wanted to come back to Burnett County."

"But if they just moved here, why aren't we bringing food to *them*?"

"Maybelle's living with her grandaddy and grandmama." Anders drawled out the words, as though explaining to a child. "Her Papa's out looking for work on the railroad."

"How old is she?" asked Kate, thinking she probably knew.

"Twelve, thirteen," Anders told her. "Used to be in our class at Spirit Lake. Too bad we don't have school again until April. That right, Erik?"

As Erik slowed the horses, he ignored Anders. Up until now Kate had been sorry there'd be no school until spring term. In that instant she changed her mind.

"Yup, that's the way it is," Anders went on. "Maybelle's been missing her good friends in Burnett County."

The red moved from Erik's neck into his face. "Aw, go jump, Anders," he growled. "Jump in a lake—a frozen one!"

Stopping the horses, Erik seemed glad for the excuse to swing down and tie them to a rail.

While Anders waited in the sleigh, Kate followed Erik up the path to the house. Ever since she'd known him, Erik had paid special attention to her. But now Kate felt uneasy.

Who is this Maybelle Pendleton? she wondered again. Kate had the feeling she didn't want to know.

3

Stretch!

$\mathcal{T}$he farmhouse door opened as though someone had watched for them. No grandparent stood there, but Maybelle herself. Kate didn't have to be told.

"Erik!" the girl cried out, and again Erik flushed red, almost as red as the girl's long braids.

Kate had always liked Lars' hair, and Maybelle's braids were an even deeper color—a red Kate couldn't describe, even to herself. She only knew she had never seen such thick beautiful hair.

"Maybelle, this is—" Erik stumbled over the words. "This is Kate—" He stopped as though trying to remember Kate's last name.

Then he grinned, seeming relieved to come up with it. "Kate O'Connell." His voice sounded too loud. "This is Maybelle Pendleton."

For the first time since Kate had known him, Erik seemed tongue-tied. Already Kate wished she'd never heard of Maybelle Pendleton. When Kate tried to smile, her face felt stiff, and her words sounded stiffer. "Pleased to meet you."

"Glad to see you back, Maybelle," said Erik, no longer stumbling.

"Come in and warm up," Maybelle told them, but she looked only at Erik.

"Oh, we're not cold," Kate answered quickly. "We're going to Josie Swensons'. We're almost there."

"But Anders might be cold." Erik didn't look at Kate. "Bad leg and all. Yup, I'm sure he's cold."

Before Kate had time to move, Erik called out, bringing Anders to the house.

Inside, the air felt warm and more welcoming than Kate liked. Maybelle's mother and grandparents were visiting a neighbor, but Maybelle stirred together cocoa, sugar, and milk. She set the kettle over the hottest part of the cookstove.

Kate dropped into a chair, but her gaze followed Maybelle. As the girl moved around the kitchen, she looked sure of every step, sure of everything she did, sure of herself.

Maybelle was slender and of medium height. Her eyelashes were dark and her eyes a deep brown. But most startling of all was Maybelle's hair. Kate wondered what to call it, even to herself.

As the boys talked with Maybelle, Kate thought about it. Then she remembered. Before marrying Papa Nordstrom, Kate's mother had been a dressmaker in Minneapolis. Once she described a dress the color of Maybelle's hair. A rich reddish brown. Russet. That's what Mama called it. Russet! The color of oak leaves in autumn.

Maybelle laughed then, a soft, tinkly laugh like a spoon against a glass. The boys laughed with her, and Kate realized she hadn't heard what was said. Nor had she spoken since entering the room.

Maybelle didn't seem to mind. As soon as the cocoa was ready, she poured it into a teapot. Returning to the table, she carefully filled Erik's cup. Then she circled the chairs to pour cocoa for Anders and didn't spill a drop.

Yet when Kate lifted her cup, Maybelle reached across the table, pouring quickly. Hot liquid shot over the top of the cup, streaming into Kate's lap.

Kate leaped to her feet, holding out her dress and sputtering.

"Oh, I'm sorry!" Maybelle's voice sounded as sweet as honey dripping from the comb. "Did I hurt you?"

"*Hurt me? That cocoa's hot!*" Kate held the front of her skirt away from her body.

"Oh, Kate, forget it!" exclaimed Anders. "Maybelle couldn't help it."

"It was just an accident," Erik chimed in.

But Kate looked up into Maybelle's dark eyes—eyes that didn't look nearly as sorry as the sweet voice sounded. In that instant Kate felt sure Maybelle had spilled the cocoa on purpose.

"An *accident*!" Kate exclaimed, waving the front of her skirt back and forth. "Ha!"

"Stop it, Kate!" said Anders, his voice low.

Kate's temper flared. "*I* stop it? *She* started it!"

Both Anders and Erik looked embarrassed. As Maybelle went to the stove, Anders pinched Kate's elbow. For the first time since she'd known him, he looked shocked at her behavior.

"Kate, mind your manners!" he whispered hoarsely.

Kate flipped her long braid over her shoulder and glared at Anders. Just the same, she sat back and struggled to keep quiet. *Don't they really know what Maybelle's doing?* she wondered.

Maybelle smiled sweetly, looking down her nose as though unable to understand this strange, backward girl. Erik and Anders stared at Kate as if she'd lost her mind.

After that, even the boys were ready to leave. Kate felt glad. She could hardly wait to get out of the house and away from Maybelle. But as they started toward the door, Erik turned back. "Why don't you come with us to Swensons'?"

Maybelle didn't take even a minute to pull on her coat and mittens. As Erik walked and Anders hobbled down the path, Kate knew she hadn't won after all.

When Maybelle reached the sleigh, she jumped up to the place between Erik and Anders. Kate grabbed the heavy robe and threw it onto the straw behind the seat.

Climbing up over the end of the sleigh, Kate circled the food. Her wet skirt slapped against her legs. She'd be cold the rest of the ride, but her misery went deeper.

As Erik started the horses, clouds scudded across the sky. Before long, the clouds darkened and slipped over the sun.

Kate grew even colder. Shivering, she pulled the robe over her head. Even then she heard Maybelle talking to the boys.

The road to Josie's seemed to last forever. Chilled to the bone,

Kate promised herself one thing. She'd get to see Josie's vanishing kitten. Since the mother cat's death, Josie had fed the kitten to keep it alive.

Kate had finally warmed up when she felt the sleigh make a turn. Like a turtle coming out of its shell, Kate poked her head from beneath the robe. Standing up, she looked over the high board sides of the sleigh. The horses had entered Swensons' driveway.

Just then a very tall man came out of the house. He bent his head in order to clear the door.

"Big Gust!" Kate cried, breaking her long silence.

The tallest man in all of Wisconsin, Big Gust stretched up to seven and a half feet. When he straightened, the top of his head reached far above the door. As Grantsburg's village marshall, he had helped Kate and Anders more than once.

Then someone else joined Big Gust on the porch. A thin boy with curly hair. Stretch!

Older than Kate, Anders, and Erik, Stretch had a bad reputation. Usually he grinned and looked as though he owned the whole world. Now the tall blond boy glanced toward the sleigh and drew back, almost behind Big Gust.

The village marshall put his large hand on Stretch's shoulder. He seemed to wait for Kate and Maybelle and the boys.

Kate jumped down from the sleigh. Her wet dress clung to her knees. Underneath her wool coat, the skirt felt clammy.

When Kate first met Stretch at Spirit Lake School, she had liked him. Most of the other children did too. But not Anders. Anders and Erik had never trusted the tall blond boy. Because of them, neither had Lars.

Now Kate dreaded talking with Stretch. When she reached the porch, he appeared even more embarrassed than she felt.

"Hi, Kate," he said, seeming to force himself to speak. His eyes shifted, looking away.

"Hi, Stretch," she answered and wondered what to say next.

Big Gust helped her out. "Stretch and I had a good Christmas together."

Stretch looked up at the giant and grinned. "Yup! Your *little* sister is a great cook!"

"Yah," answered Big Gust with his Swedish accent. "You'll get some flesh on your bones while your father's gone."

His hand still on Stretch's shoulder, the marshall turned to the others. "Mr. Swenson asked Stretch to stay here while he works for them."

"*Here?*" asked Kate, the words spilling out before she thought. "Stretch will stay at *Swensons'*?"

A shadow flickered across Stretch's face. Once again he edged back.

Instantly Kate regretted her words. Big Gust reassuringly slapped Stretch's shoulder.

"Going to turn over a new leaf, this boy is. Going to get his life straightened out and make something of himself."

Stretch grinned. As the shadow left his eyes, Kate remembered why she had first liked Stretch.

Now he seemed to believe the marshall's words could come true. But then the tall boy looked at Anders.

Instead of saying hello, Anders deliberately turned his back. The shadow returned to Stretch's eyes.

In that instant Kate forgot her wet dress. She even forgot how she felt about the way Maybelle treated her. Instead, Kate wished she could make things right between Stretch and everyone else.

Just then Mr. Swenson came out of the barn, carrying some long poles. Seeing him, the marshall left them. "Promised I'd give Henry a hand."

Anders grinned. "Any hand Big Gust gives will be mighty big. Let's take a look."

Grabbing his crutches from the sleigh, Anders swung off. The others followed.

Across the yard Mr. Swenson and two neighbors stood near a small log building. As Kate and the others watched, one man slid the end of a strong pole under the building. Another man rolled a round log into place. Using the log as a fulcrum, the men pushed down on the pole. Nothing happened.

"What are they doing?" asked Kate.

"Trying to move that building," Erik told her.

"Just a minute," Mr. Swenson called out as Big Gust reached them. "We've got some good help."

Seeing the marshall, the men grinned and stood back.

Big Gust strolled over to the building. Looking as if he used no effort, he pushed down on the pole. That side of the building moved up, a foot off the ground.

Anders laughed. "No trouble at all!"

"Hold it!" Big Gust told the two men.

Taking positions on either side of Gust, the two men held down the pole. The marshall let go. The end of the pole flew up with the men still hanging on. As they dangled in midair, the building crashed to the ground.

Once more Big Gust took his place and pried the building up. As the men came beside him, Gust called the boys. "Come here! Lend a hand!"

Anders swung himself over, then dropped his crutches, and balanced on one foot. Erik and Stretch followed, taking places on the pole beside the men. The five of them held the pole down and the building up. Big Gust slipped a heavy timber for a skid under that side.

As the building settled onto the skid, the giant went around to the other side. Once more Big Gust slid a pole underneath the bottom log. Moving slow and easy, he pushed down and lifted that side. Before long, it too rested on a skid. The building was ready for horses to drag it across the snow.

The hard work done, Big Gust waved goodbye and drove off.

Mr. Swenson turned to Anders and Erik. "Can I help you with something, boys?"

Anders shook his head. "We came to help *you*." Swinging across the yard, Anders led Mr. Swenson to the sleigh.

Everyone followed but Stretch. When Kate glanced back, he stood a short distance away, listening.

"We brought this," Anders said proudly. "It's from all your neighbors." Leaning into the sleigh, he picked up one of the frozen packages of meat, carefully wrapped in newspaper.

"For me?" asked Mr. Swenson, seeming unsure what to say.

"Not just that piece," said Erik. "All this." He pointed to the sleigh, filled with meat and other kinds of food.

"For us? Yah?" Mr. Swenson couldn't seem to believe such great blessing. "For my family? *Tack! Tack!*"

His words sounded like the tock of a clock, but Kate knew it was the Swedish "thank you."

"To make up for the steer that was stolen," said Anders.

Out of the corner of her eye, Kate saw Stretch stiffen. As she turned, he glared at her with angry eyes.

In the next instant Stretch whirled around. With long strides he headed for the barn. When he reached the door, he didn't look back.

4

The Unwanted Visitor

Kate stared at the ground, wishing she didn't have to look at anyone. The silence grew long.

"What's wrong?" asked Maybelle. But no one answered.

"Stretch has his pride," Mr. Swenson told her at last. "But he'll make a good man, that boy. Yah, he'll make a good man."

"Stretch?" Startled, Kate looked up. Much as she wanted things to go better for Stretch, she found it hard to believe he'd become a good man.

"Yah, *Stretch*," said Mr. Swenson, his voice firm. "Yah, certainly," he repeated, making sure Kate understood. "If we believe in him, he'll make a good man. You'll see. And I want the three of you—Anders, Erik, and Kate—to help him."

Ignoring Maybelle's puzzled look, Mr. Swenson turned back to the sleigh. "Now. My family and I say *tack*. It is too much. Too much. We thank you with all our hearts."

If he'd had a suit coat on, he would have bowed, Kate felt sure. Instead, Mr. Swenson went to each of them in turn. When he came to her, Kate's small hand felt lost in his big one. Mr. Swenson shook it heartily.

"Matilda!" he shouted. "Come, Matilda! Meat for winter! Meat from these good boys!" He glanced at Kate. "And this good girl."

Not only Mrs. Swenson, but a line of children tumbled from the house. Smiling shyly, Josie led her eight brothers and sisters.

Kate knew some of the children from school, but it was the first time she'd seen all of them together. Standing in a line, they looked like stair steps, each a bit shorter than the one before.

Beaming with pride, Mr. Swenson introduced them to Kate and Maybelle. "You know Josie."

Josie smiled shyly at Kate but only nodded in Maybelle's direction. In her arms Josie held a small calico kitten.

"Jacob and Joshua, Jonah and Jesse," said Mr. Swenson, as each child stepped forward. "Jethro and James."

Mr. Swenson paused for breath. A little girl was next in line. "And this is Rebecca." With light brown hair, hazel eyes, and freckles across her nose, she looked like a three-year-old Josie.

"Ah, and here is Jennifer," said Mr. Swenson, turning toward his wife and the baby she held.

"You are too kind, bringing all this food!" cried Mrs. Swenson. "It is too much! Too much!" Her eyes shone with gratitude.

Erik and Josie's older brothers helped Mr. Swenson carry the meat to the summer kitchen. Used for cooking during hot weather, the small building was not heated during winter. The meat would stay frozen until spring.

Kate followed Josie into the farmhouse. The main floor looked like two rooms set together in a T. The top part of the T, originally a log home, was now a large sitting and eating area. The later addition, a big kitchen, extended out behind. Along the wall where the two rooms met, a stairway rose to an upper floor of three bedrooms.

Cold from her wet dress, Kate went over to the wood cookstove. Stretching out her fingers, she warmed her hands.

Josie showed her the new kitten. Calico had gray, white, and orange markings and green eyes. As Kate stroked the soft fur, the kitten purred.

Kate scratched her gently between the ears. "This is the vanishing kitten? She looks too happy to disappear."

"Calico likes you!" Josie laughed, handing the kitten to Kate. "But wait a bit. If anything scares her—"

Just then Josie's three-year-old sister came into the kitchen.

"Be kind to the kitty, Becca," Josie told her.

The little girl touched the kitten lightly. "Pretty. Kitty pretty."

Taking one look at Becca, Calico nestled deeper into Kate's arms. Kate stroked the kitten's back until Calico grew quiet.

"Let's have milk and cookies," Josie said, and Kate moved away from the stove. As she sat down, the kitten settled into her lap, purring softly.

A moment later, Maybelle came to the door. Calico lifted her head and looked around. The next instant she leaped to the floor and streaked into the front room.

Kate jumped up and followed, but the kitten was nowhere to be seen. "Where'd she go?" Kate asked Josie. "How can she disappear like that?"

The two of them searched under and behind every piece of furniture in the large open room. They looked around the chimney and large heating stove and beneath the nearby shelves. Kate even checked the branches of the Christmas tree standing near a window. But they found no trace of the kitten.

"See what I mean?" asked Josie. "Every now and then she just vanishes."

Kate found it hard to believe the kitten was really gone. "Can Calico get outside? It's awfully cold, and if she'd couldn't find her way back in . . ."

Josie looked worried. "That's what scares me. But I can't find a hole anywhere. I don't know how she'd get out." She nodded toward the front door that led outside from the sitting room. "See? It's closed."

"Is there anywhere else we can look?" But even as Kate asked, she knew they'd checked every possible place.

Josie led Kate back to the Christmas tree. "I want to show you something." Reaching under the branches, Josie picked up an opened gift, still within its newspaper wrapping. "Look what I got for Christmas!" She held up a long wool scarf. "Mama knitted it for me."

Seeing the deep red scarf, Kate felt happy for her friend. "What a beautiful color!"

Josie stroked the soft wool. "And I got an apple and candy from the party at church. What did you get for Christmas?"

Kate had received both a scarf and mittens, plus a sheet of organ music and an apple. She didn't want to make her friend feel bad. "You'll look really nice in that color," Kate answered quickly, hoping Josie wouldn't ask again.

In that moment Maybelle and the boys came in and joined the search for the kitten. They had no better success.

But Kate didn't want to give up. "If Calico was outside all night, would she freeze to death?" Kate asked.

"Yup," Anders told her. "If she didn't find a warm place. Or a wild animal might get her."

Erik glanced toward Josie. "But the kitten's not outside. All the doors are closed."

Seeing Josie's face, Kate realized her mistake in asking. She tried to comfort her friend. "And the doors were closed when Calico disappeared."

Josie's hazel eyes with long dark lashes still looked worried. "Well, we've got another mystery to solve. Maybe you can figure out this one too."

"The case of the vanishing kitten!" Anders joked.

Yet Kate felt uneasy. She liked Calico and didn't want harm to come to her. "She's just a baby kitten. Where could she possibly go?" Deep inside, Kate wondered, *Is there a little hole somewhere—a hole where Calico gets outside?*

A moment later sleigh bells jingled in the yard. A matched pair of gray horses pulled a new cutter up to the hitching rail.

Through the window Kate saw a man jump down from the small sleigh. Beneath his sealskin cap his hair looked newly trimmed. A thick mustache covered his upper lip. As he tied the grays to the rail, his long raccoon coat swung open to reveal a black suit.

For a moment the man looked around as though liking what he saw. Then he started toward the house.

"Oh no!" muttered Josie. "Leonard Harris. I have to get Papa."

Hurrying into the kitchen, she slipped out the back way.

A moment later the man pounded on the front door.

Drying her hands on her apron, Mrs. Swenson hurried into the room. Pausing a moment, she drew a deep breath, then opened the door. "Hello, Mr. Harris."

"Hello, Mrs. Swenson. And where is your good husband?"

"Soon he'll be here." Mrs. Swenson sounded breathless. "Come in, come in."

Removing his sealskin cap and the long raccoon coat, Mr. Harris handed them to Mrs. Swenson. As he sat down, he looked around, again appearing to like what he saw.

Why does he act as if he owns everything? Kate wondered. In his handsome face, the man's eyes seemed cold.

A moment later Mr. Swenson came in. He offered his hand to the stranger. Yet Mr. Swenson's smile looked stiff. When Kate, Anders, Erik, and Maybelle went into the kitchen, the door closed firmly behind them.

Whatever Mr. Harris needed to say did not take long. Within five minutes Kate saw him stroll to his cutter, a satisfied smile on his face. As his horses left the rail, a large black whip snaked out, snapping above their heads.

Several more minutes passed before the door into the kitchen opened. As Josie came through, Kate heard Mrs. Swenson's stout voice. "Yah, we pray."

Josie's face looked pinched and white, as though she were holding back tears. "That awful Mr. Harris wants to take our farm," she whispered, her voice rising in desperation. "And Papa's afraid he will!"

5

Josie's Secret

*W*ho is Mr. Harris?" Kate asked Josie.

"A loan shark!" her friend replied. Josie's eyes sparked with anger.

"What's that?" asked Kate.

"A crook," Erik told her. "If someone lends money, he charges interest to pay for the use of that money. But a loan shark charges a really high rate of interest."

"And makes it hard to pay back a loan?" asked Kate.

"Makes it *impossible*!" Erik exclaimed, sounding worried. "People lose their farms."

Kate wondered if Erik was thinking about his own family. A few months before, Lundgrens had been forced to move into the small house near Spirit Lake.

"Does your father have any money at all?" Kate asked Josie.

The other girl shook her head. The anger in Josie's eyes was gone now, replaced by misery. "I don't know what we'll do. If we don't make a big payment on January twenty-fifth, Mr. Harris will take our farm."

"That's less than a month away!" cried Kate. She, too, felt scared and angry.

That night she fell asleep thinking about Josie and her family.

The next morning Kate woke up feeling awful. At first she wondered what had happened. Then she remembered Mr. Harris and his spotless black suit. She remembered how he looked around, as if he already owned everything the Swensons had.

Compared to that, the way Maybelle acted didn't seem important. Yet Erik had always been Kate's special friend. Didn't he feel that way anymore?

Each time Kate thought about it, she hurt inside. In a tiny hidden-away spot, she ached as though she had a bad tooth.

About ten o'clock that morning Erik knocked on the door of the Windy Hill farmhouse. "Let's go skiing," he said, and all of Kate's hurt disappeared.

"You know I can't," grumbled Anders.

"But Kate can." Erik grinned at her. "Let's go."

Kate could hardly wait to get outside. During the months since Erik had made skis for her, she'd become fairly good on them.

Quickly Kate pulled on her warm coat, long scarf, and mittens. The day seemed bright and wonderful. Maybe she'd imagined the way Erik acted toward Maybelle.

"Wait a minute," Anders called as they headed out the door. "I'll ride Wildfire. Let's find out how Josie's doing."

While Erik led the mare out of the barn, Kate slid her boot inside the strap of a ski. Erik had made the straps from old harness and used buckles. On one ski the thin metal was bent out of shape.

Carefully Kate pulled the strap through, trying not to put pressure on the buckle. Then she watched Erik slip a bridle onto Wildfire's head.

The mare looked black and sleek, her socks white and clean. In November Papa had taken their big work horses to logging camp. During these months Wildfire provided their only transportation, except for walking.

Anders planned to ride bareback. Erik rolled a stump over to his friend.

Using Erik's shoulder, one crutch, and his good right foot, Anders lifted himself onto the stump. When Erik brought Wildfire alongside, Anders managed to get on the mare's back. Erik handed up Anders' crutches.

As Wildfire set out, Anders' bad ankle jounced against the horse. Kate saw Anders grit his teeth and guessed he felt pain. But Anders kept going. Wildfire tossed her head and pranced across the yard, her tail flying.

Here on the edge of the steep hill near the farmhouse, Kate gazed across Rice Lake. Beyond the snow-covered hills lay the town of Trade Lake.

Still farther away, four miles from the farmhouse, was the settlement of Four Corners. Each week Kate walked there to take organ lessons. On days like this it seemed entirely possible she would be a great organist, the way she planned.

Erik strapped on his skis and started down the steep track to Spirit Lake School. Kate bent her knees, ready to follow. For a moment she felt a jab of fear. Yet she'd taken this hill more than once. Her hands swinging free, she swooped down the path.

Anders followed, walking Wildfire. At the bottom of the hill, the wind off Rice Lake had blown the track clean. Where it was bare of snow, small stones stuck up from the dirt, catching Kate's skis.

Beyond Rice Lake, they came to woods. When they reached the far side, Erik twisted around. "Let's take a shortcut across this field."

Ahead of her, Erik circled the drifts, finding places where the snow was less deep. Each time he took a hill, Kate skied in his tracks. But then they came to the biggest hill of all.

Standing at the top, Kate looked down, once more afraid. She waited until Erik reached the bottom of the hill, then skied into position. Again she looked down. Long and steep, the hill fell away more sharply than anything Kate had tried.

Erik looked back. "You can do it!" he called.

Kate stood there, trying to build up her nerve. The hill seemed to drop into nothing. Her knees felt weak.

Anders rode up behind her. "What are you, a scaredy-cat?"

That did it. Taking a deep breath, Kate crouched and pushed off.

The wind rushed past her, cold upon her face. Partway down the hill, Kate felt excited. It almost seemed as if she were flying.

Then her right ski slipped too far out. As Kate pulled her foot back, something felt wrong. Arms waving, she fought to keep her balance. In the next instant the ski slid away.

Frantically Kate swung her arms. She felt herself falling forward. She'd go head first down the hill!

Fighting against it, Kate leaned back. For a moment she wobbled and almost went over. Somehow she steadied herself. Holding out her arms for balance, she straightened her right leg and bent her left, crouching down on one ski.

Again Kate wobbled and almost went over. Regaining her balance, she stayed upright until the bottom of the hill. There she sprawled into soft snow.

Emerging from the drift, Kate wiped snow from her eyes. "I did it!" she exclaimed. "I *really* did it!"

But when Erik reached her, he looked concerned. "Are you hurt?"

"Not a great skier like me!"

"You *are* great!" Erik exclaimed. "I don't know how you did it. But are you all right?"

Looking up into Erik's eyes, Kate felt good. He really cared what happened to her. "Yup," she answered.

Erik gave her a hand up. "You're sure?" he asked.

Kate laughed. "Never been better."

"Good show, Kate!" called Anders, riding up on Wildfire. "Greatest show on earth."

Kate brushed the snow off her long stockings. Somehow she'd lost her mittens. Already her hands felt icy cold.

Erik rescued them from a snowdrift, then asked, "What happened?"

"I don't know." Kate bent down to brush off her coat.

Erik found her missing ski against the trunk of a small pine. "Uh-oh, here's the problem. It's that old buckle I had to use. It broke, and the strap fell apart. But I can't fix it here."

"Let's go to Maybelle's and get warm," suggested Anders.

Though her feet were numb with cold, Kate pulled back. "Let's go home instead."

"It's too far," Anders insisted. "And we all need to warm up."

But Erik surprised both of them. Swinging Kate's skis across the mare, he set them on top of Anders' crutches. "I'm going home," Erik said. "I know where I can get a new buckle. Then Kate can ski back."

Maybelle met Kate and Anders at the door and soon had cocoa ready. This time Kate took no chances. She waited, warming up by the cookstove, until Maybelle poured the cocoa. Then Kate sat down at the table.

"What happened?" Maybelle asked.

"Kate was just trying to show off," Anders told her, winking in his sister's direction.

Kate didn't think it was funny. "You know better, Anders Nordstrom!"

"Now, Kate," Maybelle told her, "you don't have to worry when he talks like that. You just get nice and toasty warm."

Maybelle's honey sweet voice made Kate feel sticky all over. Tossing her head, Kate flipped her long black braid over her shoulder.

When at last Erik returned, he held a shiny new buckle in his hand. He gave it to Kate. "I couldn't find a strong enough needle to sew it on."

"Let's go to Josie's," said Anders. "Her father will have what you need."

Instantly Kate grabbed her coat, but Maybelle followed them again. When they got to Swensons', Josie surprised them. She looked like a different person. Even her eyes sparkled.

"Did Calico come back?" Kate asked.

Josie nodded. "But not 'til after dark. I get scared every time she disappears. I'm afraid something will happen to her."

When the boys left to search out Mr. Swenson, Josie, Kate, and Maybelle went into the large room. Becca came from the kitchen.

Looking up at Kate, she held out Calico. "Pretty kitty?"

Kate set the buckle on a low table and took the kitten. Cradling it in her arms, she sat down. As she stroked the soft fur, Calico tucked in her paws, wound her tail around her body, and purred.

Becca picked up the shiny buckle. "Pretty?"

"Pretty," said Kate. "Can you say *buckle*?"

When Becca left, Kate and Josie and Maybelle tried to talk. Yet even to Kate's ears, they sounded stilted and uncomfortable, as though trying to think of something to say.

Strange, Kate thought. *Usually Josie can't talk fast enough.*

Today she seemed to talk around everything Kate wanted to know. Whenever she looked at Maybelle, Josie seemed troubled.

Then Kate remembered. Josie and Maybelle had known each other before Maybelle moved away. Had Josie learned she couldn't trust the other girl?

Erik and Anders returned without finding either Mr. Swenson or a strong needle. When Maybelle joined the boys in the kitchen, Josie whispered in Kate's ear.

"I have to talk to you."

Kate's heart thumped. Only a few months before, Josie had spoken those same words. That time Swensons' steer had been stolen.

"Something else wrong?" asked Kate. The loan shark still weighed heavy on her mind.

But Josie's face seemed to shine. "Yesterday when Big Gust talked to Papa and Mama about Stretch, they asked him to stay here," Josie explained. "After Stretch went outside, I heard Papa say to Mama, 'Matilda, I know we made the right choice. Stretch needs help. But he'll eat big. He'll eat like a man.'

" 'We did the right thing, Henry,' Mama said. 'God will take care of us.'

" 'Yah, he's never let us down,' Papa answered. 'But the steer we raised is gone. And in just one month we must make that big payment.' "

A tear slid down Josie's cheek. "An hour later you and Erik and Anders drove up with the food."

Kate swallowed. Much as they had wanted to help, none of them had any idea what it would mean.

Reaching out, Josie took Kate's hands. "Close your eyes." Josie led Kate across the room. "Promise to keep a secret?" she asked.

Kate nodded.

A moment later Josie put something in Kate's hands. "Open your eyes."

Kate looked down to a small square box.

"It came this morning," Josie explained. "It was supposed to be a Christmas gift, but didn't get here 'til today."

"What is it?" asked Kate.

"If I show you, you mustn't tell anyone." Josie's voice was so low that Kate could barely hear. "Promise?"

"I promise. No one else knows?" asked Kate.

"Just my family. And Stretch, because he was here when it came."

"But what is it?" Kate asked.

"It came from my grandpa in Sweden. Along with this letter."

Josie and Kate sat down on the floor in a place with a good view of the kitchen door.

"I've heard the story since I was a little girl," said Josie. "But I'll read the letter." Unfolding a small piece of paper, she translated the Swedish words for Kate: "Dear Henry—"

"That's Papa," Josie explained, then continued reading:

> "When you were just a boy, I told you the story of this ring. My grandfather—your great-grandfather Joshua—was a hero. One night when out walking, he passed the estate of a wealthy landowner. He saw flames coming from the roof. He woke everyone and got them to safety, master and servants alike.
>
> "As they stood outside, the landowner discovered his youngest daughter missing. Joshua ran back in, passed through the flames, and carried the girl out in his arms.
>
> "The grateful landowner asked, 'What can I give you?'
>
> "Joshua shook his head. 'Anyone would have done the same.'
>
> "But the landowner pulled a ring off his own finger.
>
> " 'You saved my daughter's life,' he said to Joshua. 'This ring is very valuable. Someday you may be in want, and it will save your family.' "

Josie looked up, then went on translating the letter. "Then Grandpa writes":

> "I am an old man. I don't need the ring anymore, but you have many children. Keep the ring if you can, in honor of a brave man, your great-grandfather Joshua. But if you are ever

in need, find an honest man. Sell it, and use the money to help your children."

Josie looked around to be sure no one could hear. Kate's gaze followed hers. Through the kitchen doorway she saw Maybelle laughing with Erik and Anders.

Carefully Josie opened the box. Inside was another smaller box, and she opened that also. On a silk lining rested a gold ring set with many precious stones.

Kate gasped. "Are those diamonds?" When Mama was a dressmaker in Minneapolis Kate had seen diamonds now and then. Some of the fine ladies wore them.

Josie nodded. "And rubies. Papa says all of the stones are very valuable."

The diamonds and rubies caught the light from the window. Seeing their sparkle, Kate almost felt afraid. "What will your father do with the ring?" she asked.

"He plans to find an honest man, sell the ring and make that big payment," Josie answered. "Papa says there might be enough money to pay off the farm and buy machinery and tools. He said, 'Maybe it will even be enough to help other boys like Stretch.'"

"Your papa cares that much about Stretch?" asked Kate.

Again Josie nodded. Her eyes seemed nearly as bright as the diamonds.

Kate reached out and squeezed her friend's hand. "I'm really glad for you, Josie."

"I knew you would be, Kate. That's why I told you. But remember, it's a secret. Papa doesn't want anyone to know something so valuable is here."

"A secret," promised Kate, her voice low. "It's safe with me."

But then Kate looked beyond Josie to the doorway. Maybelle stood there, her eyes wide.

How long had she been listening?

6

Howls in the Night

How much did Maybelle hear? Kate wondered as she brushed her long hair.

Over a week had passed since Kate had seen Josie. The New Year had rolled around with 1906 becoming 1907. Now as Kate got ready for church, questions still whirled in her head. *Was Maybelle listening when Josie talked about that valuable ring?*

Josie didn't trust Maybelle, Kate knew. Neither did she, and with good reason. It'd be a long time before Kate would let Maybelle pour cocoa anywhere near her.

Pulling back her hair, Kate worked it into a single braid. Just as she finished, she heard sleigh bells jingle. Kate glanced through a bedroom window. The Lundgren horses were crossing the field between the two farms.

That week Erik's father had gone to work in a lumber camp. Mr. Lundgren had left his big work horses behind. Kate felt glad. Wildfire could pull only a light cutter by herself, not the heavy sleigh it took for all of them to get to church.

More than that, Kate liked riding with Lundgrens. Hurrying downstairs, she passed through the front and dining rooms into the kitchen. Already the rest of the family had bundled up in winter clothing.

When Anders followed Lars and Tina out the door, Mama held back. "Be sure to tell the children about the party for Anders," she whispered.

Kate nodded. "Thursday morning. Ten o'clock."

As she closed the door behind her, Kate felt the January air nip her cheeks. Strong gusts picked up new snow, driving it in whirlwinds across the yard.

Erik's mother and sister Chrissy sat on straw in the bed of the sleigh. Anders pulled himself onto the seat next to Erik, and Lars started to follow. A knitted cap hid the tuft of red hair usually sticking up at the back of his head. He sneezed and his blue eyes watered in the wind.

"Lars?" called Mama. "Are you catching a cold? You ride back here."

Lars groaned.

"Come on! There's less wind."

Slowly Lars moved down into the straw. Kate knew there was nothing Lars wanted to do less. He'd rather be up front with Erik and Anders.

Kate took Lars' place between the two boys, and Erik flicked the reins. The big work horses headed down the track to the main road.

"Stretch said Mr. Swenson is going to teach him how to be a blacksmith," said Erik.

"Josie's father is a blacksmith?" asked Kate.

"He does that besides farming," Erik told her. "And he's a good blacksmith, Papa says. If Stretch stays with it, he'll learn a trade."

"You mean if he can manage to stay honest," Anders growled.

"Stretch will," said Kate.

Anders shook his head. "It's just his say-so that he's going to go right. Don't forget, Stretch earned his reputation bit by bit."

"That doesn't mean he can't change," defended Kate.

But Anders wasn't convinced. "I don't know why Mr. Swenson asked him to stay there. It's one thing to have Stretch work for him. He doesn't have to live there."

"Yes, he does," Erik broke in. "It's a long walk to his family's farm, especially in winter."

"I still say you can't trust him."

"Mr. Swenson asked us to," answered Kate. "He wants us to help Stretch."

"But how do we know that he's changed?" asked Anders. "What if he really hasn't? He might try to get *us* to do something wrong."

"So we get hurt?" Kate asked. She thought about the way neither Anders nor Erik seemed to realize what Maybelle was doing. "Are you wondering if we'll get hurt 'cause we believe Stretch is all right, even though he isn't?"

"Yup, you got it," said Anders.

"But what if Stretch really does want to change?" Erik shot back. "If we don't believe in him, that's terrible too!"

"So what do we do?" asked Kate. "How do we know the difference?"

For a time they were silent, thinking about it. Around them, heavy frost clung to the pine trees along the road. With each movement of the horses, bells jingled in the cold air.

At last Kate spoke. "I know. We can pray. We can ask God to show us if it's all right to trust Stretch."

Anders looked surprised at her idea. "I don't know—" he started.

But Erik grinned in agreement.

Moments later they reached the church. Anders leaned on his crutches while Erik put the team in a barn. Taking hay from the sleigh, Erik dropped it down in front of the horses.

Kate waited until Anders started talking to a neighbor. "Surprise birthday party," she whispered to Erik. "This Thursday, January tenth. Ten o'clock. Tell all the boys, will you?"

As he covered the horses with blankets, Erik nodded. Kate hurried to the church.

Near the steps groups of people shook hands and talked. "*God dag, God dag,*" they greeted one another. It sounded like "good dog," but Kate knew it was the Swedish hello.

In the entryway, a tall Swede grinned down at Lars, giving permission to ring the bell. Lars' freckled face broke into a smile.

Going to the strong rope that dropped through a hole in the ceiling, he tugged hard. The bell clanged loudly. The rope swung back up, pulling Lars off the ground.

Kate followed Mama and Tina into the main part of the church. There the women and children went to the left, the men and boys to the right. When Mama, Tina, and Kate filed into a pew, Mrs. Lundgren and Chrissy joined them. Nearby sat Josie and Becca, with Mrs. Swenson holding the baby.

Glancing across the aisle to the men's side, Kate stiffened with surprise. A tall thin boy with curly blond hair sat next to Mr. Swenson. *Stretch in church?* It seemed hard to believe. *What's he doing here?*

Seeming to sense Kate's stare, Stretch turned her way. One eyelid dropped in a long, slow wink. Kate jerked her head back. A warm flush crept into her cheeks.

After that she kept her eyes straight ahead, but listened to the organ. In Minneapolis she'd been able to watch the organist. Here he sat in the balcony.

When everyone stood for the first hymn, Kate sneaked a look back. Was Erik up there, pumping the big handle up and down, bringing air into the organ? Kate couldn't tell for sure. But she knew the hand-pumped organ well. It was the one on which she took lessons.

As they sang the first hymn, Kate listened to every note. *I'll be a great organist someday,* she told herself, as she had many times before. For many years she'd admired Jenny Lind, the Swedish nightingale. Kate hoped to travel around the country giving concerts the same way. Instead of singing, Kate would play the organ.

Pastor Nelson wore a black suit with a stiff white collar. When he started preaching, Kate wished she understood his Swedish words. Standing in the big pulpit, he seemed far away. Yet Kate knew he loved young people. Erik had told her so, and Erik knew him well.

Before long Kate's mind drifted. She glanced across the aisle to where Stretch sat with Mr. Swenson. She remembered talking to Anders and Erik. "Help us, God," Kate prayed silently. "Help us know if we can trust Stretch."

Then Kate thought about the hymns they'd sung. She let the songs play over and over in her mind. She wanted to remember every note so she could play them on her own organ.

As soon as the service ended, Kate found Josie. Looking beyond her friend to where Anders stood with a group of boys, Kate lowered her voice. "Birthday party for Anders. Thursday. Ten o'clock. Be sure everyone knows it's a surprise."

"I'll tell all the girls," said Josie.

Kate knew Josie would look forward to the party all week. "Tell 'em to come early so they can hide."

"Is Anders going to be away, so we can sneak in?"

Kate grinned. "As my brother would say, 'Yup!' He doesn't know it yet, but he will be."

Josie laughed, and Kate looked back to the group of boys. Seeing Erik there reminded her. "You know the buckle Erik gave me? I forgot it at your house yesterday. On that low table."

"I'll bring it Thursday," Josie promised.

Then Kate realized something was wrong. Already the sparkle had disappeared from Josie's eyes. She looked worried as she glanced over her shoulder toward the boys. Stretch's blond curly head was there now, too, but turned away.

"How come he's in church?" asked Kate, her voice soft.

"Papa asked him to come. Said he expects it of anyone living with us. And when spring term starts, Papa wants Stretch to go to school."

"To *school*?" Kate found that hard to believe.

"Papa told him he needs more education. That he needs to finish eighth grade."

"Even though Stretch works for him?"

"Papa says that's one of the good things about America. The chance for people to get ahead."

But Kate knew there was still something Josie wasn't saying. "What's the matter?" Kate asked.

Josie dropped her voice to a whisper. "The ring is missing."

Kate's heart thudded into her stomach. "Missing?"

"Nowhere to be found."

"But it was there just before we left."

"I know," sighed Josie. She darted a quick look toward Stretch.

Kate had a different thought. "Your brothers or Becca wouldn't take it, would they?"

"Of course not!" Even the idea upset Josie. "All of them are honest. But that leaves just one person."

"Two," said Kate. "Don't forget Maybelle. Anders says her parents need money. More than usual, I mean."

Josie shook her head. "I don't think she'd take it. But blaming Stretch bothers me even more. When he came to live with us, Papa said we should believe Stretch when he says he wants to make good."

"Your papa told us almost the same thing." As she spoke, Kate remembered her prayer. "Can I tell Erik and Anders about the ring?"

"I asked Papa. He said, 'Yah. Maybe they can find it for us.' But Kate, we have to find it soon. In less than three weeks Papa has to make that big payment. If he can't, we'll lose the farm."

Soon after, Kate's family left for home. During the ride, the wind whipped up. Sitting in front again, Kate spoke softly, telling Erik and Anders about the missing ring.

"It's Stretch," said Anders, his voice low. "He took it."

"Why do you think that?" asked Kate.

"Who else would? All the boys in the family are too young. Besides, they wouldn't steal from their own father."

"But that doesn't mean Stretch would take something," said Kate.

"Doesn't it?" asked Anders. "How do you know?"

"Why can't it be someone who doesn't live in the house?" Again Kate thought of Maybelle.

"Nope," said Anders. "It's Stretch. I'm sure it's Stretch."

All afternoon the wind blew, holding the farmhouse in an icy grip. Even a few feet away from the wood stove, the walls felt drafty and cold.

Darkness fell early. By the time Kate went upstairs, Tina was asleep. Strong gusts swooped around the corners of the house. Windows rattled. In the light of the full moon, pine branches tossed up and down. On the frosted panes, their shadows became pointing fingers.

Blowing out the candle, Kate crawled into the bed she shared with Tina. But the long dark shadows still waved up and down.

Kate closed her eyes, trying to blot out the pointing fingers. In the next moment she heard a howl in the distance.

Clutching the quilts, Kate pulled them over her head. She stuffed fingers into her ears. Even so, the eerie sound reached her. From far away a howl started low, rose and fell, then lingered in the night air.

Kate's muscles tensed. She had never seen wolves, but it wasn't hard to imagine them gathered in a circle, noses pointed at the moon. Another howl followed the first, echoing through the countryside.

Then, as Kate listened, the wolves moved closer.

7

The Search

Somewhere near Windy Hill Farm, a wolf answered.

In the darkness Kate trembled. She wanted to wake Tina and ask, "What should we do?"

Reaching out, Kate poked her. The little girl moved away and slept on.

"Tina!" Kate whispered, but her sister rolled over.

Once again Kate nudged her. This time Tina didn't even wiggle. Her breathing sounded deep and even.

Kate felt silly, wanting help from a five-year-old. Yet Tina had grown up on the farm. She'd know what to do. She might even say, "Oh, Kate, go to sleep!"

Right now that seemed like something Kate wanted to hear. Instead, she lay awake a long time. Each time a wolf howled, she shuddered, feeling more afraid.

When Kate awoke the next morning, the wind had died down. Sunlight streamed through the windows, slanting across the bed.

Monday, Kate thought. *No school!* No school until spring term started on April eighth. One moment Kate felt glad. The next minute she wished she could see Josie and her other friends every day.

51

Then Kate remembered the wolves. Though the sky was blue and the day bright with sunshine, she felt afraid. She had no idea how long she had listened to the wolves howl.

Trying to push aside the memory, Kate scrambled out of bed, dressed, and went downstairs. When she reached the kitchen, she found Mama sitting at the table.

Usually her mother piled her golden blond hair high on top of her head. This morning it still hung in one braid down her back. It made Mama look young and helpless, but Kate knew better. Though Mama wasn't as strong as most farm women, she wasn't helpless. On the table in front of her lay an open Bible.

Mama saw Kate and smiled. But Kate had seen the lonesome look in her mother's eyes.

When Mama started to get up, Kate noticed the growing bulge under her mother's big apron. Gently Kate pushed her back into the chair. "I'll get it. What do you want?"

Mama lifted her cup, and Kate took the pot from the cookstove. As she poured out the coffee, she saw it wasn't steaming. Lifting the stove lid, she put in small chunks of wood, then set the pot over the firebox.

After breakfast Anders had an idea. "Let's go over and see if we can help Josie."

"I can't ski," said Kate, as she remembered the broken buckle.

"You don't have to. We can ride bareback on Wildfire."

Kate helped Anders with the mare's bridle. She led the horse to a stump, and they both managed to get on. Anders held his crutches in front of him, across Wildfire's mane.

The winter air was crisp and the sky without clouds. As the mare plunged through a drift, snow sprayed up. "Good thing you've got Wildfire," Kate said.

"Yup," Anders agreed. "Would be pretty hard getting along without her. Got any ideas about the ring? Or how we can help Josie's family?"

"Let's start by searching the big room," Kate answered.

Windy Hill Farm, Erik's house, and Swensons' farm were located on the three points of a triangle. Crossing the field, Kate and Anders rode through the woods to Lundgrens' house. From there Erik skied alongside them. Before long they passed Spirit

Lake School and came to Swensons'.

Josie met them at the door. Her eyes looked scared. The house seemed strangely empty with everyone else outside.

When Josie took them into the large open room, Anders asked, "How did your father get mixed up with that old loan shark?"

Josie's hazel eyes sparked with anger. "When Papa first came from Sweden, Mr. Harris was nice to him. He told Papa where there was land and how to get to Burnett County. He said, 'If you ever need money to get started, let me know. I'll help you.' "

"So Mr. Harris isn't from around here?" asked Kate.

Josie shook her head. "When Papa found this farm, he asked Mr. Harris for a loan. Papa was so new to America, he didn't understand that the interest was far too high. Even before we had a big family, he and Mama struggled to make payments."

"Has your father missed payments?" Erik wanted to know.

Again Kate remembered how the Lundgren family had lost their farm.

"Papa got behind when our steer was stolen," Josie told Erik. "He had planned to sell part of the meat. And once he got behind when Mama was sick.

"But he paid later?" Erik asked.

Josie nodded. "Papa wanted to go to logging camp this winter. But there's too much work to leave Mama alone."

"So we *have* to find the ring," said Anders.

"Without it, Papa doesn't have a way to make that big payment." Josie turned to Kate. "And I can't find your buckle."

"That's all right," Kate told her. Without the buckle she couldn't ski, but compared to losing a farm, skiing didn't count. "Let's start hunting for the ring."

Josie showed the boys the two boxes and described the ring. Together they searched the big room.

While Anders and Josie worked as a team, Kate started by peering behind the large heating stove. Erik helped her lift all the wood from the nearby box. Next they searched around the large oak table, and under every chair.

At last they reached the wall next to the kitchen. Shelves stretched between the door and the chimney. The top shelf was above Kate's head and the lowest close to the floor.

Erik stood on a chair and searched behind the few books on the highest shelf. Kate carefully picked up the wooden bowls and tin cups on lower shelves.

When they'd covered every inch of the room, Kate asked, "What about the kitchen?"

"Mama and I looked through everything this morning," Josie said. "And I mean *everything*!"

As Anders dropped down on the floor, he bit his lip as though feeling pain. Kate knew he was growing tired.

"Is there any other place we can look?" Erik asked.

"What about outside?" Kate wanted to know.

"That's hopeless," Josie told her. "What could we find in the hayloft? Or the granary and chicken coop? All of them have a million places to hide something."

"Wait a minute," said Anders. "We've got to use our heads. Who would want the ring most? And where would he hide it?"

A shadow crossed Josie's eyes. "I don't like what you're saying, Anders."

"Well, what about Stretch? What if he has it? What if some night he took off with it?"

"It'd be gone forever." Josie sounded miserable.

But Anders kept on. "Where does Stretch sleep?"

"Upstairs," she told him. "With all the other boys in one big room."

"Where's Stretch now?"

"Out in the blacksmith shop, working with Papa."

Anders grabbed his crutches and lifted himself up. "How about if I look through Stretch's things?"

8

City Girl Farmer

*A*nders started for the door.

"No, Anders. You can't." Josie's hazel eyes were still shadowed, as though filled with pain. But her voice sounded firm. "You aren't going up there."

"Why not?"

"Papa says we're supposed to trust Stretch."

Anders faced her. "Well, it won't hurt to just have one look."

"Yes, it will," said Erik. "It's saying we don't believe he started over."

Just then Josie's mother came in from collecting eggs. "Do you know where Becca is?"

Kate jumped up. "I'll go look. Is she outside?"

"Try the blacksmith shop first. Stretch is good to her. She follows him around to watch what he's doing."

Pulling on her coat, Kate hurried out. She wasn't sure where the shop was, but it wasn't hard to guess. Set closest to the road, the building was off by itself with the door open in spite of the cold.

Becca stood just inside, watching her father and Stretch. Seeing the older girl, she reached up and tucked her hand inside Kate's.

Within a large stone forge a fire burned brightly. Stretch stood nearby, opening and closing the big bellows. With each whoosh of air the fire burned hotter. Even here by the door Kate could feel its heat.

As Kate watched, Mr. Swenson told the blond boy what to do. Stretch took a large tongs and lifted a cherry red piece of iron from the fire. Putting it on the anvil, he picked up a heavy sledge. The shop rang with his measured pounding. Gradually the hot iron took the shape Stretch wanted.

Mr. Swenson nodded his approval. "Good. Good. You've almost got it. Just a little more now."

Just then Stretch glanced up. Seeing Kate, he looked embarrassed, but kept working.

Mr. Swenson glanced toward the door. "Got a good blacksmith here," he told Kate. "He's already got a strong arm."

Stretch kept pounding. When he looked Kate's way again, a glimmer of pride had replaced his embarrassment.

What's it like? Kate wondered. *How does it feel having to make good when you've got a bad reputation?*

A moment later Stretch dropped the hot piece of iron into a bucket. As the cold water sizzled up, Kate took a guess. *It's probably like being new at school. Only worse.* It wasn't hard remembering how it felt to be a stranger, left out and alone.

In that instant Kate made up her mind. She flipped her long black braid over her shoulder. Afraid she'd lose her nerve, she spoke quickly. "Stretch, would you like to come to a birthday party for Anders?"

Stretch looked up, surprise written across his face.

As he glanced toward Josie's father, Kate asked, "Would it be all right, Mr. Swenson? Can Stretch take some time off?"

For a moment Mr. Swenson looked at him, then back at Kate. "Yah, it'd be all right. It might be good for Stretch to have a few hours off." Mr. Swenson winked at the tall boy. "He'll work even harder when he gets back."

Stretch grinned.

"Thursday. Ten o'clock. And it's a secret," Kate told him. "Be sure you come early so you can hide while Anders is gone."

As Stretch returned to his work, Kate left the blacksmith

shop. Starting back to the farmhouse, she thought about her invitation to Stretch. Already she felt scared. Now, when it was too late, Kate felt sure she'd done the wrong thing. Though she wanted to help Stretch, Kate knew Anders would not be pleased.

A half hour later, she and Anders and Erik left Swensons'. On the way home, Kate kept thinking about the party. *What if the others don't accept Stretch? He'll feel even worse.*

When Kate and Anders reached Windy Hill Farm, Mama was coming down with a cold. She looked tired and moved more slowly than usual. Her waist was straight up and down except for the bulge out front.

Three months now, maybe four until the baby comes, thought Kate. *What will it be—a brother or a sister?* With all her heart Kate wanted another sister. But she knew Anders wanted a boy.

That afternoon the supply of wood was low. The box near the cookstove, as well as the one next to the larger heating stove, was nearly empty. Usually Anders and Lars worked together to split wood and bring it in. Today Lars started carrying wood by himself.

Anders sat at the kitchen table, his bad leg stretched across a chair. He glanced up from reading the *Journal of Burnett County.* "Farmers are going to have a meeting on January twenty-second," he said. "They want to get telly-fones out in the country. To every farmer."

"Tell-*eh*-phones," said Kate, correcting Anders. She'd seen telephones in Minneapolis, though she'd never used one. *What would it be like being able to call Josie?*

On his second trip to bring in wood, Lars sneezed. He blew his nose and went back out. Returning with a third load, he dropped it quickly into the wood box. As he covered his nose with his hands, he sneezed again.

Mama looked up from where she kneaded bread. "Are you getting another cold?"

Lars nodded and sneezed at the same time. His blue eyes watered.

Mama sighed. "You can't keep going in and out. Your colds turn into coughs too easily. Kate, will you bring in the wood?"

"There's no more to carry," said Lars. "It needs to be split."

Dragging himself to his feet, Anders reached for his crutches and swung over to the door. Dropping down on a bench, he pulled on Papa's old work boots.

The first boot fit easily on Anders' large foot. As he tried to slip the second boot over his bad ankle, he winced. The ankle was still too swollen.

Anders set down the boot and pulled on the large wool sock he'd been wearing over his other stocking. Picking up his crutches, he hobbled outside.

Soon he returned, looking discouraged and upset. "I can't do it!" he exclaimed.

"Don't be too hard on yourself," said Mama. "I don't know of anyone who splits wood standing on one foot."

"But if I don't split it, who will?" asked Anders. "I hate it when I can't do things—especially things I do well!"

"I'll help," said Kate, even though she wondered if she could. She followed Anders out to the woodpile. Logs of various sizes, sawn into shorter pieces, waited to be split.

Most of those pieces were too heavy for Kate to lift. Choosing the smaller ones, she rolled them over to Anders, and tipped them with the sawn side up. As she stood back, Anders swung the axe, splitting the wood as many times as needed.

Often he needed to sit down on a log and regain his strength. "I can't believe how long this is taking!" he exclaimed once when he staggered on his good foot. That time he leaned against a shed.

"Believe it! Believe it!" teased Kate.

Yet she saw her brother in a new way. *It seems to matter a lot to Anders that he can do whatever he sets out to do.* Tall, with strong muscular arms, he usually had no problem with anything he tried.

As soon as Anders split a pile of wood, Kate carried armloads into the house. Slivers of wood stuck to her mittens. Bits of dirt and sawdust soon covered the front and arms of her coat.

Before long, Kate's shoulders ached. She felt silly with weariness. Coming back outside, she watched Anders. "What's that bird that stands on one foot? A crane?"

Anders grinned, as though guessing how ridiculous he

looked. After that the work seemed to go easier.

The rest of the day dragged by as Kate helped Mama with first one thing, then another. With relief Kate watched the sun slip over the horizon. The short winter afternoon had seemed years long.

When Tina set the supper table, Kate dropped into a chair. As she buttered her potatoes, she saw Mama look hard at Anders.

Kate's gaze followed Mama's. Around the edge of his face Anders seemed pale—almost as pale as on the day he sprained his ankle in the woods. Through her tiredness, Kate felt uneasy.

Mama waited until they finished eating. "Anders, I think I better take a look at your ankle."

"I'm doing fine," he answered quickly.

"You're just pale for no reason?" she asked.

"Really, Mama, I'm fine."

Kate snickered. She knew a Swede could be almost dead and yet say, "I'm fine."

"Yah, maybe so," Mama told Anders. "But maybe not. So let me see."

Anders pushed back his chair and reached down. Slowly he worked off his wool sock. More than once he flinched.

Kate took one look at his ankle and bit her lip to keep from crying out. The ankle was blue and black and purple. Deep marks showed where the sock had pressed into the badly swollen flesh.

Kate could barely stand to look at it. She felt sorry she had snickered.

As Mama checked the ankle, gently feeling it, Anders clenched his teeth. Even Mama's careful touch seemed painful.

Her voice sounded sharp with concern. "Anders, you stood too long today. You have to get your leg up. Keep it raised so the swelling goes down."

Anders grinned weakly, as though trying to hide how he really felt. "Sure, Mama. Soon as I milk the cows." Slowly, carefully, he eased on the sock he usually wore, then reached for the heavier, outside sock.

Mama wasn't going to be put off so easily. "Anders, I want

you to teach Kate how to milk the cows."

"Oh, Mama!" Kate cried out. "I'm a girl. You don't *really* expect me to—"

"Yah, I expect you to milk them." Mama spoke in her no-nonsense voice.

"That's not girls' work," said Kate. "It's for boys!"

"Kate!" Mama's voice was the sharpest Kate had heard in some time. "If you'd grown up in Sweden, you'd know better. In Sweden milking is women's work."

"But, Mama, this is America!"

"It's America, all right! And we all work together! Lars can't do it, and Anders needs help."

Kate sighed loud enough for Mama to hear. Just the same, Kate knew she had no choice. She put on the overalls she wore for beekeeping, then her coat. Anders swung himself through the snow on the beaten-down path to the barn. Longing to escape the work ahead, Kate followed.

Once there, Anders hobbled over to pick up a three-legged stool. "Miss O'Connell, this is your equipment." His voice sounded dead serious. "You must always take good care of this stool."

"Oh, stop it!" Kate snapped.

Anders smirked. "Now I know that you don't take your work seriously, but it's very important that you do."

Kate glared at him, but Anders seemed not to notice.

"Upon you we rely. Without milk we will not have our daily bread."

"Our bread?" Kate laughed.

"Yup," Anders told her, his voice solemn. "Our food. Without you, we will not have milk for our oatmeal."

"That wonderful oatmeal I like so much!" Kate answered.

Anders paid no attention. "Without you we will not have milk for our cheese. We will not have butter for our lutfisk."

"*Lute fisk?*" Kate drawled out the word, wrinkling her nose. She hated the smell of the dried cod that Swedes soaked in lye and ate at Christmas.

Just then Anders' dog brought the last cow into the barn. In winter the animals stayed closer to the barn, but Lutfisk still felt it necessary to nip at their heels.

Seeing the dog, Kate said, "You sure gave him a funny name. Just because he got into the lutfisk!"

Anders whistled, and Lutfisk immediately came to him. Dropping his crutches, Anders knelt down.

The dog had brown and black hair with white and tan markings on his face. Resting one of his paws on Anders' sleeve, Lutfisk gazed up, waiting. Anders scratched behind the dog's ears.

When Lutfisk dropped back to the dirt floor, Anders again took up his role as teacher. Using his crutches, he swung himself over to the cow farthest to the left. She stood next to the high board wall that separated the stall from a walkway.

Patting her wide back, Anders chained the cow to a board in front of her. "This is Clover," he said. "Clover, meet Kate."

The Holstein turned her head as though understanding. In that moment Kate realized how big the animal was. The black blotches on her white side seemed to stretch out forever. Kate was short for her age, but felt even smaller next to Clover.

"First you set the stool on the cow's right side," Anders went on in his solemn voice.

Thinks he can trick me, Kate told herself, remembering how she needed to approach a horse on its left. *Well, I'll fool him!*

Picking up the stool, she set it down on Clover's left. But as Kate walked into the stall, the cow stomped her hind leg.

Kate jumped back, away from the hoof. Once again, she looked up at the big cow. Its black and white side towered above her. Yet, not for anything would Kate let Anders see her fear. *He'll call me scaredy-cat.*

Moving forward, she started to sit down.

In the next instant the cow stepped sideways, pinning Kate against the high wall.

9

Wildfire!

$\mathcal{K}$ate beat her hands against the cow's side, then shoved with all her strength. After a very long moment, Clover stepped away. Quickly Kate retreated, far back of the cow's rear hooves.

Anders snorted. "You didn't believe me, did you? And I was trying to help you! Go to the left of horses, to the right of cows."

Her heart in her throat, Kate reached forward and picked up the stool. Carefully she settled herself on Clover's right side.

"Now I'll show you what to do," said Anders, again solemn. Reaching across Kate, he began milking the cow. "Like so."

In that instant the whole thing struck Kate funny. She giggled. "If Sarah Livingston could see me now!"

"Who's Sarah?"

"My best friend in Minneapolis. Before I came here, she told me what it'd be like living in the wilderness. She warned me about the bears and wolves. She said there'd be log houses with the wind blowing through."

"Anyone who makes a good log house knows enough to fill the cracks," Anders said stiffly. "Besides, people are starting to put siding on them. Now pay attention."

But Kate giggled again.

"Look," Anders sounded like a teacher. "First you close one hand, then another. At the same time, you let up or tug down."

Kate's shoulders shook with laughter.

Anders stepped back. "If you think it's so funny, try for yourself!"

"Oh, anyone can milk a cow!" replied Kate.

Picking up the pail, she put it between her knees as she'd seen Anders do. As she reached forward, the pail dropped, rolling onto the dirt floor.

Anders shook his head. "Dirty pail, dirty milk." He took down a second pail from where it hung on a nail in the log beam. "Now keep this one clean."

Carefully Kate put the pail between her knees and turned back to the cow. Just then Clover flicked her tail, swatting Kate in the face. She jumped, and the second pail rolled to the ground.

"Awww, Kate." Anders sounded disgusted. "Even a city girl can do better than that."

Again he took down a pail. "Last one we've got. Now keep it clean."

Kate nodded solemnly, starting to realize milking might not be so easy, after all. Reaching out, she tried to milk the cow. Nothing came.

"Do it again," insisted Anders.

Once more Kate tried. Once more nothing came.

"I said this isn't girls' work!" Kate exclaimed. She was starting to feel sorry for the cow.

Anders groaned. "Stand up!" he said. He dropped onto the stool with his bad leg sprawled out along the side of the cow. "Now keep your eyes open. By this time I could have finished milking every cow."

Kate's temper flared. "By this time *I* could have done the dishes and practiced my organ lessons!"

Once again Anders asked her to sit down. It took several attempts before milk trickled into Kate's pail. Yet gradually she caught on. She even felt excited at what she accomplished. Then she realized milk had flowed down inside her coat sleeves. Her arms were wet.

Going to the pump, Anders washed out the other pails and

sat down near the next cow. Immediately warm milk splashed into Anders' pail.

Lutfisk raised his head.

Moving his hands slightly, Anders aimed a stream of milk toward the dog's mouth.

Lutfisk stretched out his long tongue and licked the milk away. Walking over to a corner, he picked up a sardine can in his teeth. Returning to Anders, the dog set the can on the dirt floor and waited for Anders to fill it.

Before long, Anders had milked four cows to Kate's one. When they finished the milking, Anders looked paler still, even in the light of the lantern.

"Get the oats for Wildfire, will you, Kate?"

"Oats? From where?"

Anders tipped his head toward a walkway. "In that bin. See how it's locked? Make sure you close it the same way. If you don't, Wildfire will lift the cover with her nose."

Kate dipped out the oats and carefully locked the bin. As she held the bucket, Wildfire snuffled her nose into the grain.

"Awful nice horse, huh?" asked Anders.

Kate nodded, hearing the pride in his voice.

"Black shiny coat. White socks and star. Yup. A real pretty mare."

"Teach me to ride her, will you, Anders?" Kate had learned to hitch Wildfire to the cutter, the small sleigh used for only a few people. Twice she'd ridden bareback with Anders, but she'd never taken the mare by herself.

"Nope," said Anders.

"Why not? You taught me how to hitch her up."

"You can't ride her."

"Aw, Anders, come on. If you let me, I'll take some of your turns watching Tina."

But Anders refused. He led Kate out to the large tank for watering animals. Set inside was a stove that heated the water during winter.

The tank heater looked like a U with the sides pushed slightly down. At one end of the U a stovepipe stretched above the water. At the other end was an opening to load wood.

Dropping his crutches, Anders lifted the stove lid and pushed in kindling and small chunks of wood. Then he dropped a lighted splinter down the chute. As Kate watched, the fire caught the wood at the bottom.

"In this weather we have to keep the heater going all night," said Anders.

"Or the water will freeze?" Kate asked.

"Big chunk of ice in the morning."

When the fire burned well, Anders told Kate to load more wood from a nearby pile. Then he returned to the barn for one more look at Wildfire.

Kate followed. "Why can't I ride her?" she asked again. "Give me one good reason."

"You betcha," said Anders. "You don't know how to take care of her."

"You could teach me."

"You have to take mighty good care of a horse. If you don't slow her down after a run, she'll founder."

"Founder?" asked Kate.

"Get sick. You have to rub her down if she gets sweaty. And you have to watch how she eats. If Wildfire ate too many oats, it would affect her circulation. She'd get stiff in her legs."

"Crippled?" asked Kate.

Anders nodded. "Crippled for life. Or she could die." Anders rubbed Wildfire's nose. "Yup. Got to take awful good care of you."

Suddenly Kate felt chilled. She looked around, but the door of the barn was closed against the wind. Even so, as Kate watched Anders with his horse, she felt uneasy. He'd worked hard to get the mare. Wildfire meant a lot to him.

Thinking about it, Kate knew the mare meant a good deal to her too. She tried to push aside the awful thought that came to her mind. *What if something happened to Wildfire?*

10

Race Against Time

I'll take really good care of Wildfire, Kate promised herself. *I'll make sure nothing happens to her.*

Yet Kate's uneasiness wouldn't go away. During the evening she thought more than once about her brother's mare. *What would we do without her?*

How Anders would feel was bad enough. But the only other horses nearby belonged to Lundgrens. In winter their farm was a long cold walk through the woods.

At the same time, Kate longed to ride Wildfire. The next day Kate asked Anders again. Once more he said no.

As the icy winter days passed by, Mama kept a close eye on Lars and his cold. Anders favored his ankle and often propped it up. The bluish purple color faded into yellow and light green. Gradually the swelling went down.

On the January afternoon before Anders' party, Kate walked the long wagon track to the mailbox. When she reached the main road, she found a letter from Papa. Feeling she'd discovered a treasure, she walked fast or ran all the way home.

When Mama saw the letter, she settled herself into her favorite chair. Her eyes shone with happiness. As all of them gathered around, Mama's skillful hands fumbled, awkward in her eagerness to open the letter.

Papa had written in Swedish, and Mama began reading aloud. Tina leaned forward on Mama's knee. Anders and Lars moved closer. But Kate edged back.

I'm trying to learn Swedish, thought Kate. *But everyone else spoke it 'til they started school. Doesn't Mama remember how little I know?*

Kate felt separated from the others. Restlessly she pulled even farther away.

Mama noticed her. "I'm sorry, Kate. I forgot." Returning to the first page, Mama translated Papa's words into English. "Papa says he had a safe trip back. No problems with the weather. Wages are good this year."

As Mama read, her gaze moved quickly across the page. Her words sounded sure and strong. Then she reached the place where she'd gone back to translate.

"Papa talks about his camp. It's up in the heavy timber. Some of the white pine are four feet across. Now and then, even five feet."

As though she were thinking, Mama slowed down. Her gaze darted ahead. When she started translating again, Mama stumbled over the words.

At first Kate thought Mama was in too much of a hurry, wanting every bit of news about Papa. But her mother's gaze seemed to move faster than she spoke. Kate felt uneasy.

What's Mama doing? Kate wondered as she twisted the end of her long braid. *Is she skipping parts of the letter?* There were too many words for the amount Mama translated.

Just then Anders stood up. Looking over Mama's shoulder, he read the letter to himself. Anders could read Swedish as well as English. He'd know what Papa said.

And Kate would do her best to find out.

As she climbed the stairs that evening, Kate thought about Papa's strange letter. Why didn't Mama read all of it aloud?

Though tired from everything that had happened that day, Kate couldn't go to sleep. Turning this way and that, she puffed her pillow and slid deep beneath the warm quilts.

It was no use. Kate's thoughts went round and round. Josie's vanishing kitten, the valuable lost ring, the missing buckle.

Then Kate remembered Papa's letter. The more she thought about it, the more awake she became. What bothered her most was how Mama seemed to skip certain parts.

Anders knows. Whatever is wrong, he knows what it is, Kate thought. Beneath the shock of blond hair, his blue eyes had looked worried. Just like Mama's.

Finally Kate gave up trying to sleep. Her thoughts turned to a piece of Mama's good brown bread. Kate knew how tasty it would be, covered with freshly churned butter.

Pulling on her robe, she tiptoed down the steps, through the front room, and into the dining room. Mama's bedroom was off the dining room. Kate crept even more softly, trying not to wake her mother.

As Kate reached the door to the kitchen, the clock chimed ten times. To her surprise Kate saw Mama sitting at the table. For a moment Kate stood near the doorway, watching her.

Wisps of golden blond hair hung down over Mama's forehead, making her look soft and unprotected. Yet there was something more in her face, something Kate wondered about. *Is Mama afraid?*

Her slim hands held a letter that looked like the one from Papa. Mama's lips moved, as though memorizing every word.

As Kate watched, a tear slid down Mama's cheek onto the page. Carefully Mama blotted it dry.

Then Kate heard someone at the outside door. Quickly Mama pushed her hair into place and wiped the tears from her cheeks.

Kate stepped back, out of sight. Yet she knew by the sound it was Anders, leaning his crutches against the wall. Kate edged farther into the dining room. *Why is he still up?*

"Everything all right?" Mama asked Anders, but her voice quavered.

"Yup! Sheep are snug as a bug in a rug."

Kate wondered if he was trying to sound cheerful for Mama's sake. She heard Anders move over to the cookstove.

"Needs more wood," said Mama, her words ragged as though trying to stay calm.

A stove lid clanked, and Kate knew Anders had lifted it to push in chunks of birch.

"Coffee?" he asked, and Kate didn't need to see. Mama would lift her cup while Anders poured steaming coffee into it.

A chair scraped. Anders must have sat down across from Mama. After a long silence he spoke. "I saw the rest of the letter."

"I thought you did," answered Mama. She lowered her voice, and Kate strained to hear. But she couldn't catch Mama's words.

"Papa will be safe," Anders told her, and Kate wondered if he talked to himself as much as to Mama.

"But he said—" Mama changed into Swedish.

English, Mama, Kate wanted to shout. *English!*

When Anders spoke again, he also used Swedish.

Mama sniffled and blew her nose. The sound frightened Kate even more than the words she didn't understand. Mama never cried except for something really serious.

What are they talking about?

Then edging through Kate's fear came another feeling. Mama and Anders seemed like two friends as they sat there together. For the second time that day Kate felt left out.

One part of her mind wanted to walk in and say, "Tell me too." The other part remembered how much Mama hated eavesdropping. She didn't want Kate listening in when other people talked.

Careful not to make a noise, Kate stayed out of sight. For a long time she listened, but Mama and Anders never returned to speaking English. Only once did Kate recognize a word, and that word was *wolf*. Even the sound of it frightened her.

Soon after, Kate heard one chair, then another, scrape across the kitchen floor. As footsteps neared the doorway where she stood, Kate raced for the stairs. At the top she tumbled into her bedroom, closing the door just as Anders started up.

Panting and out of breath, Kate leaned back against the door. She thought hard. *Whatever is wrong, Mama doesn't want me and Lars and Tina to know. Why? Why did she tell Anders and not me?*

To find out Kate would have to get Mama alone.

———

The next morning Kate entered the kitchen planning to ask Mama about the letter. But Tina and Lars were already there, helping Mama get ready for the surprise party.

Kate knew Anders wouldn't expect a party. Children seldom had them, and if they did, their friends didn't bring presents. But Mama wanted to celebrate Anders' thirteenth birthday. Kate hoped it would be a great surprise.

They waited with eating until he came down for breakfast.

"Happy Birthday, Anders!" cried Tina, her blue eyes sparkling.

Lars grinned at his brother, and Kate started the singing.

Mama's good wishes were also warm. At the same time, she seemed unprepared for the big day. "Oh, Anders, I need some sugar," she said. "Will you ride to Olsons' for me?"

Behind Anders' back, Kate grinned at Lars. Mama hadn't lied. She needed sugar, all right, but only because the cake was already made and hidden away.

Kate and Mama had worked out a plan to get Anders away from the farm while his friends slipped into the house. No one would walk on the road coming from Olsons'.

So far everything was going perfectly, and Kate knew she should be happy. Yet she couldn't get Josie's family out of her mind. When her friend came today, what would she say about the missing ring?

Slowly Kate stood up, dreading the idea of milking the cows alone. Yesterday morning Lars had been well enough to muck out the barn. Today he was worse again.

Kate trudged outside. *I need to hurry,* she thought. *I want to be ready before anyone comes.*

But nothing went right. When Kate tried to milk Clover, the big cow moved restlessly. Then Kate realized she hadn't fed her.

Setting down the half-filled pail of milk, Kate climbed the ladder to the loft. She gathered armloads of hay and threw it down into the walkway around the large open stall.

Returning to the main floor, she spread the hay in front of the cows.

Clover edged forward. As she chomped her large teeth, her brown eyes rolled at Kate. Kate edged back out of the way.

Clover tossed her head.

"Laughing at me, are you?" asked Kate.

Then Kate found three cats standing on their hind legs, drinking milk out of the pail she'd forgotten. "Scat!" Kate cried, and they did. But they also tipped over the pail. The milk poured out, mixing with the dirt floor to become mud.

With a long *moooooo* Clover turned her head toward Kate. "You *are* laughing at me!" she exclaimed.

Everyone will come by 9:30, she thought. *Josie and Erik might be walking here now.* Quickly Kate dipped out oats for Wildfire, then threw hay into the sheep pen. Usually she talked to the sheep. Today she hurried on, eager to be done.

Once more Kate went back to milking. Each time she filled a pail she poured it into a larger, covered pail. It was going better now, and Kate felt sure she could finish in time. She even felt proud of all she'd learned about taking care of the animals.

If Sarah Livingston could see me now! Kate thought, as she had many times before.

She was milking the last cow when Lutfisk picked up the sardine can between his teeth. Setting it down next to Kate, he woofed.

Moving her hands as Anders did, Kate tried to direct milk into the can. Missing, she tried again. Each time the milk shot outside the can onto the floor. Finally Kate stopped, tipped her pail, and poured milk into the sardine can.

Just then the cow stomped her back leg. Jerking sideways, she hit the bucket. The rest of the milk splashed out on the floor.

Kate jumped to her feet. Losing her balance, she sat down hard.

One moment she felt herself on the dirt floor. The next instant she scrambled up. Yet it was too late. Her boots, coat, overalls, and hands were covered with mud.

Just then Kate heard the barn door open. "Kate?"

Uh-oh! Erik! Frantically Kate looked down. From head to toe she was wet and dirty.

Grabbing a handful of hay, she tried to wipe off the mud. Instead, the hay stuck to her wool coat, adding to the mess.

"Kate?" Erik called again.

Kate ran toward Clover. Brushing past the cow, she slipped into the dark space next to the high board wall. In the dim light Kate hoped the shadows would hide her.

11

Kate's Choice

A moment later Erik found Kate. "How you coming with the milking?"

"Just finishing up." She breathed deeply, trying to catch her breath.

"Your mother says you've been here an awful long time."

"Not so long," Kate told him, trying to keep her voice steady. She didn't want Erik to know how hard it was for her to milk all the cows.

City girl, Anders calls me. Kate hated to admit he was right. At the same time she felt proud she'd learned as much as she had.

"What's the matter?" asked Erik.

Kate swallowed. Not for anything would she tell him about the milk she'd spilled or how she'd fallen on the dirt floor. Nor did she want Erik to see how awful she looked. Kate tried to edge farther into the shadows.

"I'm almost done," she said, wishing he'd leave. More than anything in the world, she wanted to get cleaned up.

"I'll help you finish," Erik offered, moving closer. "Everyone will be here soon."

"No!" Kate burst out. "I'll do it myself!"

Erik stepped back. "Well, you don't have to get mad about it!"

"I'm not! I mean, thank you—I mean, I'll finish up as soon as you leave."

Erik looked hurt. "I just wanted to help."

"You did. I mean, you have. You are."

"I'll take the milk in."

"No!" Kate burst out again. He'd guess how much she'd spilled.

Erik stared at her strangely. This time he moved beyond Clover to the space where Kate hid. For the first time he had a good look at her.

As the corners of his lips turned up, Kate glanced down at her filthy clothes. The shadows weren't enough. They didn't hide the mud that covered her from head to toe.

Erik slapped his hand against the stall and bent over laughing. The sound seemed to echo through the barn.

A hot flush crept up into Kate's neck, then warmed her cheeks. Slowly she walked out of the stall.

In the light from the open door, Erik studied her face. The laughter died on his lips.

"Kate," he said, sounding as if he were trying to be serious, "you've got only a few minutes." But his voice cracked.

Erik took a deep breath, as though trying to straighten his face. "Everyone will be here. Don't you think you ought to get washed up?" In spite of himself, he grinned, then choked.

Kate fled to the house, wondering if she'd ever forget the sound of his laughter.

Reaching the back door, she crept into the kitchen. As she pulled off the boots she wore in the barn, clumps of dirt fell on Mama's clean floor. Kate pushed the boots under a bench. Hanging her mud-spattered coat on a peg, she wanted only one thing: to wash up and change before anyone else saw her.

A basin filled with clean water waited for her. Leaning forward, Kate splashed water onto her face, then gasped. The water was icy cold. Mama must have set it out some time before.

Kate shivered, knowing she had no choice but to use it. She

plunged her hands and arms into the basin. Grabbing the bar of soap, she rubbed at the dirt.

Each time the water touched her skin, Kate flinched. The cold water seemed to smear the dirt around. Finally Kate gave up and wiped off whatever she could on a towel.

Just then she heard a knock on the door. "Mama!" Kate yelped, running through the kitchen. In the doorway to the dining room, she met her mother. "Someone's here!"

As she fled through the front room, a girl giggled from behind a chair. Kate bounded up the stairs.

In her bedroom she pulled off her wet overalls and the dress underneath. Wrapping them in a ball, Kate hid them under her bed. Here, where the sunlight streamed through the windows, she got another look at herself. It was hopeless.

As Kate glanced through a front window, Erik's sister Chrissy came out of the woods. Before long she'd cross the field between the two farms.

Through a window on the side of the house, Kate spied Josie, Stretch, and Maybelle coming up the track from Spirit Lake School. Kate gasped. *What'll I do?*

Then, from the floor grate letting heat into her bedroom, Kate heard low, excited voices. Peering through the grate into the front room, Kate saw more children. They huddled on the floor, trying to be quiet.

Everyone's here! I'll miss the surprise!

Quickly Kate pulled her best dress over her head. Remembering her hair, she dashed to the mirror. Long strands escaped her black braid and hung around her face. Sweeping them back with a brush, Kate picked wisps of hay from the braid.

A muffled giggle drifted up through the grate as someone mentioned Anders' name.

Throwing down the brush, Kate took one more look in the mirror. This time she saw a dark smudge on her forehead. Kate wiped hard, trying to rub the mud away. Frantically she turned toward a window. Anders was coming from the barn!

Heading for the door, Kate tumbled down the stairs. In the front room, she squeezed in beside Josie and tried to melt into the shadows.

Someone laughed.

"Shhhhh! He's here!" Kate warned.

Instantly the giggles stopped.

Then Kate heard Anders talk to Mama in the kitchen. A moment later two crutches thudded across the wood floor of the dining room, coming closer.

As Anders passed into the front room, Erik jumped up. Kate and the others followed. "Surprise! Surprise!"

Anders stepped back, shock written across his face. "Surprise, all right! For sure!"

Turning, he grinned at Mama. "So you needed sugar! You just wanted me out of the house!"

"Happy birthday!" Josie cried, her hazel eyes dancing with fun.

Kate laughed with the others. It was fun seeing Anders so completely fooled. Their plan had worked!

But a moment later Kate's laughter died on her lips. From one of the corners came Maybelle. A sure-of-herself smile curled her lips. Her soft blue dress looked clean and neat and made her brown eyes shine.

Her long beautiful hair no longer hung in braids. It swung about her shoulders. Maybelle had *curls!*

Quickly Kate rubbed her forehead, hoping she'd gotten all the dirt off. At the same time she noticed the strands of hair again hanging around her face.

Maybelle laughed—the soft, tinkly laugh that sounded like a spoon against a glass. She looked up at Erik and smiled. "It was a good surprise, wasn't it, Erik?"

Kate wished she could disappear like Josie's kitten. But then Kate saw Stretch.

As the tall boy with curly blond hair stepped out from a corner, Anders saw him too. For a moment they faced each other and the air seemed to fill with sparks.

"Happy birthday!" Stretch said.

"Thanks," Anders replied. "Thanks for coming." But his voice sounded halfhearted. He turned away—too quickly.

Stretch flushed red. He didn't have to be told. Anders still didn't trust him.

I made things worse, thought Kate, forgetting the way she looked. *I made things worse for Stretch.* It bothered her.

But then Erik moved over and started talking to the tall thin boy. Soon Stretch grinned. His embarrassed flush disappeared.

A moment later Kate saw Josie's face—*really* saw it. Something was very wrong. Josie's hazel eyes no longer danced with fun.

"Did you get more bad news?" Kate asked.

Her friend nodded. "Papa talked to that old loan shark again. Mr. Harris says he won't give us any more time. He says the money has to be paid by January twenty-fifth—or else. That's only two weeks away."

"Do you have any other clues about the ring?" asked Kate. "Anything at all, even if it doesn't seem important?"

Josie thought for a moment. "Just one thing," she said slowly. "Remember the two boxes? One fit inside the other for mailing. Whoever took the ring didn't bother with the boxes."

"Were the lids back on?" asked Kate. "Or the smaller box inside the bigger one?"

Josie shook her head. "Maybe it's not important."

"Well, let's keep thinking about it," said Kate.

Just then Maybelle noticed Kate's reed organ along the wall of the front room. "Is it yours?" Maybelle asked brightly. "I can play for all of you."

"You can?" Kate blurted out.

"Of course," answered Maybelle, sounding as if everyone would be greatly honored. "I play very well."

"Just like she does everything else," said Josie softly, looking at Kate.

But Kate stood frozen to the spot, unable to speak. She knew only that she didn't want Maybelle to touch the keys. Though she couldn't put it into words, Kate knew something very special would be spoiled.

As Maybelle started toward the organ, Kate felt helpless, unable to think what to do.

But Anders hopped over on one foot, standing between Maybelle and the keyboard. "Time for games." He turned to Kate.

"You've got games planned for this party, don't you?"

Quickly Kate put two rows of wooden chairs in the center of the front room. Setting the chairs back to back, she counted to be sure she had one less chair than the number of young people.

"All right, line up for musical chairs," she told them.

They rushed forward and formed a line. Kate sat down at the pump organ and started to play.

Around and around the others walked, circling the chairs. Abruptly Kate stopped playing. Shouting with laughter, everyone scrambled for a seat.

Josie wasn't quick enough and lost out. As she stood aside, a boy pulled a chair out of the circle. Again Kate started playing. Each time she stopped, one more person was short a chair. Finally there was only one chair left for two people. Erik's sister Chrissy won.

As a cheer went up, Kate sensed that someone stood behind her. Before Kate could turn around, Maybelle spoke.

"Kate," she said in the sweet voice that carried throughout the room. "I know you'd like me to help you."

As Kate looked up, everyone seemed to turn her way.

"You missed some of the buttons on the back of your dress," said Maybelle. Reaching out, she started buttoning them.

Kate felt a flush of embarrassment start in her neck and move into her face. She turned her head, trying to see.

Maybelle tossed her curls, as though on the center of a stage. She seemed to enjoy having everyone watch. "I can't imagine how you managed to get hay in your hair." She sighed, a soft little sound, as gentle as a spring breeze.

Finishing the buttons, Maybelle picked a piece of hay from Kate's long black braid. Suddenly Maybelle yanked the braid hard.

Hot tears sprang into Kate's eyes. But when she tried to stand up, Maybelle held the braid firm. "I really want to help you, Kate," she said.

This time Kate did stand up. Jerking her braid out of Maybelle's hands, Kate faced the other girl. She wanted to slap Maybelle's face. She wanted to call her the most terrible name she could think of. A name that described how sly Maybelle was, how underhanded, and how honey smooth.

Then Kate had the name, the most awful one possible. But in that moment she saw Stretch watching.

As he waited, there was something Kate realized. *This is important*, she thought. Without understanding why, she knew. *This is important to Stretch.*

Deep inside, Kate felt afraid.

12

Out of the Darkness

*K*ate tried to push aside her panic. *How can anything I say be important to Stretch?* she wondered.

But Kate had no answer. Standing there with eyes wide open, she prayed. "Help me, God. Help me know what to do."

In the next instant Kate thought of something. *Maybelle's mean. But so what? I've got to show I'm bigger than that.*

Straightening her shoulders, Kate pulled herself up to the tallest her short height allowed. "Thank you, Maybelle," she said, flipping her long braid over her shoulder. To Kate's surprise her voice sounded normal. "Thank you for helping me."

Maybelle's soft white skin flushed pink. Surprise flashed across her face, then was gone.

Kate was glad when the games finished and she could escape into the kitchen. She longed to be away from Maybelle, away from her sugar sweet voice and her curls. Away also from the tension between Stretch and Anders.

Pretty soon they'll all leave, Kate promised herself as she carried the birthday cake into the dining room. *They'll eat and go home.*

As soon as everyone sang "Happy Birthday," Kate cut the cake. In a little while, the children started putting on their coats.

Before long, only Erik, Anders, Maybelle, and Kate remained.

Maybelle turned to Anders. "I hear you have a horse all your own. May I see it?"

"Yup," said Anders, not hesitating a moment. Never had he stopped anyone from admiring his mare.

Taking his crutches, he pulled himself up. Swinging over to the hooks by the kitchen door, he took down his jacket. Erik and Maybelle followed him outside.

Kate longed to go with them. Then she remembered the muddy boots she wore to the barn. *I wouldn't be caught dead in them*, she thought.

A minute later her curiosity overcame her pride. Trying not to touch the mud, Kate sat down on the bench and pulled on the boots. *I'll stay far enough behind so no one notices.*

But her coat was even worse. Kate cringed just putting it on.

When she reached the barn, she found Maybelle stroking the white star on Wildfire's forehead.

"Pretty good horse, huh?" asked Anders.

"She's wonderful!" Maybelle breathed.

"See how sleek her coat is?" he asked, his voice filled with pride.

"I really like Wildfire," answered Maybelle. "I'd like to ride her."

Kate spoke quickly. "Anders doesn't let anyone ride her."

Maybelle swung around. Her stare swept Kate from head to toe, lingering on her coat and overshoes.

Kate felt like a clod of dirt next to a shining piece of jewelry. Just the same she said, "Wildfire's a pretty lively horse."

"Perhaps Anders would like to speak for himself," Maybelle answered. "I'm sure he gives special friends the opportunity to ride."

Turning her back on Erik and Kate, Maybelle gazed up at Anders. "I used to have my own horse, before we moved away." Her deep brown eyes waited for his answer.

Anders looked uncomfortable. "Ah, um—"

Kate wondered if Anders remembered he hadn't allowed *her* to ride the mare. "He doesn't let *anyone*," she broke in.

"I'm sure I'm not just *anyone*." Maybelle's voice dripped with honey, but Kate thought of bees, ready to sting.

"Kate's right," said Anders. "Wildfire's a pretty lively horse."

"But I'm an expert rider," Maybelle persisted, as sure of herself as always.

Watching her, Kate wondered, *How does she do it?* Once more Kate felt like a clod of dirt, a clod stepped on and trampled underfoot.

At the same time she felt uneasy. Again she wondered, *What if something happened to Wildfire?* Kate couldn't explain her dread, even to herself. *Am I getting jumpy with all that's happened around Windy Hill Farm?*

Anders looked uncomfortable. "Well, uh, maybe."

"You know, Anders," said Maybelle, "people usually give me what I want."

Just then Kate saw Erik's face. His eyes widened as though seeing Maybelle for the first time.

But Anders still stumbled around. "Wildfire has a tender mouth—"

Kate stalked off, unwilling to watch Maybelle ride the mare. Hurrying out of the barn, Kate headed for the house, holding back the tears that pushed against her eyes. *He'll let Maybelle ride Wildfire when he won't let me?*

When she reached the kitchen door, Kate realized she didn't want to talk with anyone. Turning back, she hurried to the end of the barn away from the wagon track. In the pasture closest to the woods the sheep called out to her. *Baaaa!*

Slipping through the fence, Kate trudged to the far side of the field. The sheep huddled there, munching the grass that grew up around tree stumps.

Baaaa! they called again.

Kate waited until one of her favorites came to her. In spite of an all brown coat, he had a white triangle on his forehead. She sank her fingers deep into his thick wool.

For a long time she stayed there, close to the trees that grew along the fence line. When Erik and Maybelle left, Kate waited until Anders swung up the path to the house. Then Kate slipped into the barn. Cold and tired, she wanted a place to sort out her feelings.

Inside the barn she climbed the ladder and swung through the hole into the loft. There she settled deep in the hay. A few minutes later, she heard Anders call from below.

"Ka-a-a-ate! Ka-a-a-ate!"

But Kate would not answer. With a bad ankle Anders wouldn't climb the ladder. She waited, staring through a crack between the logs in the wall facing west. Deep red streaks colored the horizon.

Again Anders called, "Ka-a-a-ate! I know you're up there!"

She remained silent, watching the red sky change to gray.

"Kate!"

A moment later the barn door slammed.

It was growing dark by the time Kate pulled herself up and crawled over to the hole in the floor. Long shadows crept across the loft.

She was partway down the ladder when she heard a sound in the deeper shadows of the barn below. Kate stopped and listened.

A cat, she thought. *Or a cow moving. Or maybe it's the sheep.*

Once more Kate started down. She was close to the bottom when she heard another sound. This time it was near at hand, somewhere within the shadows. Was it someone barely breathing?

Kate's heart leaped into her throat. *Should I go back up the ladder?* She waited, listening.

Something was close by. Something or someone. But there in the corner of the barn away from the sun, it was dark. Kate could not see.

Then she heard yet another sound. A slight movement, near at hand. A movement so quiet she wondered if she imagined it.

Filled with panic, Kate whirled. Still she saw no one, only darkness. Only the munching of the animals reached her ears.

But when Kate tried to run, a hand reached out and grabbed her arm.

13

Papa's Strange Letter

*T*urning, Kate saw a big dark shape. Drawing back her foot, she kicked with all her strength.

"Owwww!" came a moan from the shadows. "Ow, ow, ow!"

"Anders!" Kate cried. "What are you doing here? I thought you left!"

Anders hobbled from the corner, holding his left ankle. "Wow, Kate. You deliver a mean kick!"

"Well, what do you think?" asked Kate. "If you're going to stand in the dark and scare me—"

"Stand in the dark and wait for you, you mean."

"Wait for me?" Kate scoffed. "What for?"

Anders groaned again. Hopping on his good foot, he reached a pile of hay close to a window and dropped down. "Waiting to talk to you."

"We don't have anything to talk about."

"I think we do." His voice was quieter than Kate had ever heard it. He rubbed his bad leg. "Right where I sprained my ankle. Just when it was getting better, I'll have a big bruise!"

"You deserved it, scaring me like that." Kate knew she should thank Anders for standing between Maybelle and the organ. But not now. Kate was still trembling from her fright.

Instead of answering, Anders pulled himself up, grabbed his crutches, and started for the door.

"Anders, where you going?" Kate started after him.

Her brother turned. "To the house. Until you stop acting dumb!"

Kate stopped right where she stood. In the final rays of the setting sun, she saw his blue eyes. He meant it all right, no doubt about that.

Anders' hands tightened on the crutches. "Kate, there's something you have to get straight." His voice was hard as iron, beyond teasing. "When Papa left, he told me I'm supposed to look out for this family."

Kate stared at Anders.

"Mama's having a hard time right now," he said. "We need to take good care of her."

Kate gasped and drew back. As though it happened one moment before, she remembered Mama and Anders together, talking in the kitchen. Again Kate felt left out. "So now you're going to tell me how to act with my own mother? She's *my* mama, you know, not yours!"

Anders looked as if Kate had slapped him. He drew himself up to all of his almost six feet. Flinging open the barn door, he set his crutches ahead of him. Swinging forward on the path, he moved toward the house slowly, as if in pain.

Kate had time only to wonder how much she'd hurt Anders' ankle. Then the wind pushed the door shut with a bang.

In that moment Kate didn't want to face either Anders or Mama. Instead, she lit the farm lantern, got a pail, and started milking the cows. By the time she finished, she was tired, cold, and hungry.

When Kate entered the kitchen, Mama looked up. Kate sat down on the bench near the door and pulled off her boots.

In that instant Kate recalled Anders' words. *Anders says I'm supposed to be nice to Mama. Who does he think I am? Of course, I'll be nice to Mama! She's MY mother!*

Kate still needed to know what was in Papa's strange letter. She hadn't had one moment alone with Mama. Kate felt separated from her, cut off and alone.

That night Kate went to bed wanting only to hide in the dark. Though sharing a room with Tina, Kate felt all alone.

When she heard Tina's deep, even breathing, Kate knew the five-year-old was asleep. In that instant the tears Kate had pushed down all day welled up. Filling her eyes, they spilled onto the pillow. Her feelings poured out like flood waters washing away everything in their path.

At last Kate could cry no longer. As she lay in the darkness she tried to think about the Jesus she had come to love. Right now He seemed far away. Kate couldn't feel His love.

Instead, she listened to the January wind in the tall pine next to the house. Frosted panes of glass rattled, and cold stretched icy fingers across the room. Sliding deep beneath the quilts, Kate covered her head.

A moment later she heard the sounds she dreaded. At first she pushed fingers into her ears, trying not to hear. But the howls came, even through the quilts.

Finally Kate pushed the quilts aside and listened. From far away, off in the distance, the howls started low, rose and fell, lingering in the night air.

Then, from the nearby woods, came the most frightening sound of all. An answering howl.

Kate trembled. What was it Papa had prayed for her? Hurt and cold, lonely and afraid, Kate tried to think back. At last she recalled the words: "Heavenly Father, when Kate needs to remember, remind her of thy care for her."

Kate's thoughts turned into a prayer. "What does that mean, God? How do you care for people like me?"

A moment later Kate drifted off to sleep.

The next morning Kate got up earlier than usual. She had decided what she could ask about Papa's letter. But Kate knew she had to be careful. Mama didn't like it when Kate listened in on other people's conversations. And Mama wouldn't answer questions just to satisfy Kate's endless curiosity. Often Mama told her, "Curious girls and cackling hens always come to no good end."

Kate found her mother alone in the kitchen. "Mama," Kate started out, "when you read Papa's letter, did you skip some of it?"

For a long moment Mama sat without speaking, seeming to debate with herself.

"What scared you?" Kate asked.

Mama lifted her head, as if remembering that a Swede would say "Nothing," no matter how afraid she felt.

But Kate saw Mama's eyes. "Tell me what's wrong," Kate urged.

Mama seemed to make up her mind. "Anders and I talked about it," she answered in a low voice.

Again that strange left-out feeling twisted Kate's insides. Long after going to bed, she'd thought about Mama and Anders together, not telling *her* those parts of the letter. "You talked with him, and you didn't tell me?" Kate sounded as hurt as she felt.

"He's always lived on a farm. I thought he could handle it. And he can. At least it seems he can."

"Then so can I," answered Kate. Her voice sounded strong, but her stomach tightened with wondering.

Mama drew a deep breath. "There are so many things, Kate. Papa's far away, and I can't talk to him. I'm afraid he'll get hurt. That he'll cut himself with an axe or a saw. Or a tree might fall on him."

Kate remembered her question to Papa. "When I asked, 'Is it dangerous?' he said, 'Sometimes.' That's why, isn't it?"

Mama nodded. "He never talks about that. He just plans to do the work and does it. But every now and then the newspaper tells about someone getting hurt."

For a moment Mama was silent, then went on. "In the letter Papa told me something he thought I needed to know."

Once again the fear returned to Mama's face. It reminded Kate of how her mother cried after Daddy O'Connell died. Kate remembered that loneliness well.

Mama cleared her throat. "Papa said a man butchered meat and brought it to the logging camp on a sleigh. Wolves followed the sleigh the whole way. They wanted the meat."

In that instant Kate's left-out feeling disappeared, replaced by fear. In her imagination she saw the wolves following like hungry dogs just behind the sleigh. She saw the horses tossing their heads, rolling their eyes, running to stay ahead of the wolves.

Kate swallowed. "Why did Papa tell you about it?"

"He wanted me to be aware of the danger. He said I must watch the sheep and the calves. Keep them close to the barn. Make sure they're in before dark."

Kate's stomach felt funny just thinking about it.

Again Mama cleared her throat. "Papa didn't know what it'd be like for me to hear about wolves. He knows I grew up on a farm in Sweden. But I lived in the city so long. He didn't know how afraid I'd be, thinking about *him*."

I'm scared too, Kate thought. *So awfully scared*. She seemed to see a low gray shadow creeping along the horizon. The awfulness of it filled her mind.

She reached forward and slid her hand under Mama's. That helped.

Mama's lower lip trembled. Struggling to hold back tears, Mama could not speak. When she did, it was in a whisper. "Oh, Kate, I don't know what's wrong with me. I don't want to be afraid."

Mama blew her nose and cleared her throat. "I guess it's the baby coming and being lonesome for Papa and having Anders hurt and Lars sick. I can't handle everything."

Kate moved her hand to rest on top of Mama's and squeezed hard. "Did Papa say anything more?" Her voice was as quiet as Mama's.

Tears watered her mother's smile. "Yah," she said slowly. "Something he told me to remember." Mama picked up the letter and found the place. "A verse from the Bible. First Peter 5:7: 'Casting all your care upon him, for he careth for you.' "

Mama's laugh was shaky. "Papa always knows what I need. If I throw all my worries on Jesus, I won't be so afraid, will I?"

Mama straightened her shoulders and sat taller in her chair. It was as though she'd taken the promise for herself and started believing it.

Kate wished the promise seemed real to her, too. Somehow

it didn't reach deep inside where she really hurt. Biting her lip, she looked away from Mama's eyes.

But her mother reached out. Tenderly she cupped Kate's chin in her hand. "There's something else wrong, isn't there?"

Kate swallowed around the lump in her throat, afraid to answer.

14

The Moving Shadow

*M*ama waited until Kate looked into her eyes. Kate knew she had no choice but to answer.

"Sometimes I wonder—" Kate broke off. She didn't know how to say it. Finally she came up with a question. "Does Anders help you more than I do?"

"Why, Kate, why do you think that?"

Kate looked away, afraid to tell Mama all the mixed-up feelings she had.

But Mama wouldn't let it go. "Kate, what's *really* wrong?"

"Sometimes—sometimes I wonder if—" She couldn't finish.

"Do you wonder if I have enough love for all of you?" Mama asked.

Kate nodded, still not looking at Mama.

"You know, Kate, the more children I have, the more I love *you*."

Startled, Kate looked up.

"For a time I had only one child to love—you!" Mama spoke slowly, as though thinking it out. "Now I have three more, plus this little one coming."

Mama patted her growing stomach. "Each of you is a special person, and each of you is very special to me. My love for every one of you gets bigger every day."

Suddenly Kate's eyes felt wet. "Oh, Mama!" The next moment Kate was in her mother's arms. It felt good to be there.

When at last Mama stood up to cook breakfast, she seemed to have new energy and strength. Watching her, Kate knew that Mama would face the day and be all right, even though Papa was far away.

When Anders came in, Kate was busy helping with breakfast. Anders looked at Mama, and Kate saw his relief. It wasn't hard to know that Mama felt better. Across the kitchen table, Anders grinned at Kate and winked.

So he thinks he can just tell me what to do, and I'll do it! thought Kate.

After breakfast, Anders followed her outside into the January sunlight. As they headed toward the barn, the snow crunched beneath their feet, squeaking in the cold.

"Starting the new year right, you know," Anders said.

Kate bristled.

"And as a reward for your excellent behavior—"

"Excellent behavior, all right!" Kate exclaimed.

But Anders paid no attention. "As a reward for your most excellent behavior—" He drew off his cap with a flourish. In spite of his crutches, he bowed. "As a reward I will teach you to ride Wildfire."

"You will? When?"

"Right now."

But Kate drew back, suddenly suspicious. "What's the *real* reason, Anders?"

Her brother held up his hands in mock terror.

"I knew it!" cried Kate. "Did Mama say you had to show me how?"

Anders groaned. "Can't keep *any* secrets!"

In spite of his grin, he still looked unwilling to teach her. Yet when they reached the barn, he handed the mare's bridle to Kate.

"Mama figures that sometime you might need to ride a horse," he explained. "She said, 'What if Kate would ever have to go for help?' "

Kate found the board that stuck out from the others at the

front of the mare's stall and pulled herself up. Gently she put her fingers in the open space between Wildfire's teeth and slipped in the bit.

The saddle was heavy for Kate. Anders hopped on one foot, helping her lift. He showed her how to tighten the belly strap.

Kate led Wildfire outside. There she climbed up on the stump, then onto the horse.

Wildfire pawed the snow, eager to be off. When Kate saw the distance to the ground, she felt a moment of panic.

Anders held the mare's bridle until he explained. "When you want to go left, lay the right rein over her mane. When you want to go right, lay the left rein over. Stay close by where I can see you."

At first the mare walked around near the barn while Anders gave voice commands. "When you want to stop, don't pull back hard. Be gentle on her mouth."

Kate tried it, and Wildfire obeyed.

At last Anders trusted Kate to go farther. "Nudge her sides with your heels," he said.

Wildfire moved into a trot. Kate bounced up and down, fighting the mare's stride.

"Relax!" Anders called out. "Ride with it!"

The mare moved off on the wagon track, eager in the morning sunlight.

By the time Anders called Kate in, she felt more at home on the mare and anxious to try again. Best of all, Anders seemed to be warming up to the idea of her riding his horse.

"Now rub Wildfire down. All over," he told Kate. "And give her some oats. Make sure you close the box and lock it."

Kate did exactly what Anders told her. She didn't want the mare opening the bin by herself.

That night Kate fell asleep thinking about her ride on Wildfire. It seemed more important than ever that the horse be all right.

Tomorrow she'd see Josie in church. She'd find out if Josie knew anything more about the diamond and ruby ring.

As Kate ate breakfast on Sunday morning, Anders came into the kitchen. He looked upset.

"Who's been out to the barn?" he demanded.

Kate knew that if Anders weren't on crutches, he would have stomped across the room. Instead, he hobbled over to the other side of the table. Standing directly in front of Kate, he glared at her.

Startled, Kate looked up to his almost six feet. "To the barn? Not me. I'm about ready to start the milking."

Anders turned to his little sister. "Tina, have you been out?"

Blue eyes wide, Tina shook her head so hard the pigtails flew.

Anders looked back to Kate. "Lars is still sleeping. And Mama hasn't been there. That leaves you, Kate."

"I told you, I haven't been outside this morning."

"Then what about last night? When you fed Wildfire, what did you do with the oats?"

"I shut the bin and locked it, just like you taught me. What's wrong?"

"When I went into the barn, the lid was open."

Kate's stomach tightened. She didn't blame Anders for being upset. "That's bad, isn't it?"

"It's bad, all right! If Wildfire got into the bin, she'd eat herself sick. A horse can founder that way."

"Founder?" This time it was Tina who didn't know what Anders meant.

"Get sick and die. From eating too much."

"Was she in the oats?" Kate asked, feeling scared.

Anders shook his head. "Can't tell for sure. Doesn't look like it. But, Kate—"

"I didn't do it!" she protested. "I locked the bin."

"But who else would leave it open?"

"Not me!" Kate tried to speak calmly. "Anders, you've got to believe me. I took care of Wildfire just like you said."

Anders sighed, but his voice still sounded angry. "Kate, I want to believe you. I really do. But there hasn't been anyone else around."

Kate fell silent, knowing he was right.

Soon after, Erik's family came with their team and sleigh to pick up the Nordstroms for church. At Four Corners, Erik put the horses in the barn and covered each of them with a heavy blanket.

Kate followed Mama and Tina into church. Together they sat down on the women's side.

Mama bowed her head to pray, and Kate knew she should do the same. But just then she looked around. Someone new was sitting with Josie and her mother. Someone with beautiful red hair. *Maybelle!*

All through the hymns Kate felt too upset to even sneak a look back at the organ. But then, just before the sermon, the organist played an introduction for special music. Erik began singing a Swedish folk song, "Children of the Heavenly Father."

Tina's favorite song, Kate thought as she glanced toward the little girl. Erik hadn't told Kate he was singing in church. As far as she knew, he'd never sung there before.

Erik sang the first two verses in English, then in Swedish. Kate stole a look at Mama. Her mother's eyes were wet. One tear slid down her cheek.

Kate reached out and squeezed Mama's hand. Then Erik came to the third verse: "Praise the Lord in joyful numbers: / Your protector never slumbers."

The words reached Kate, deep inside. They reminded her of Papa Nordstrom, but also of Daddy O'Connell. Long ago he had called her "my little colleen"—my little girl. Kate blinked away her tears.

I'll practice even harder, she thought. *I'll play for Erik when he sings in church.*

As soon as the service ended, Kate sought out Josie. Taking one look at her friend's face, Kate forgot everything else. Josie had been crying, too, and Kate felt sure it wasn't because of Erik's singing.

"A letter came from Mr. Harris," Josie said. "He told Papa to find another place to live."

Josie broke down. When Kate hugged her, Josie struggled to speak through tears. "It's bad enough to lose our farm. But how can we move in *January*?"

Again Kate hugged her, not knowing what else to do. Josie

was right. The temperature could easily drop to forty degrees below zero. And January twenty-fifth was less than two weeks away. Where would Swensons go?

At last Josie stopped weeping.

"We'll search your barn," promised Kate. "We'll look in the granary. We'll look *everywhere*! Somehow we'll find that ring! Your family has to have it!"

"Who has to have what?" asked Maybelle, coming up behind Kate.

Kate turned toward the sweet voice. In the light of the window, Maybelle's soft skin and red hair looked more beautiful than ever.

But Maybelle paid no attention to Kate. Instead, she spoke to Josie. "My mother says I can take organ lessons again."

Josie choked.

Maybelle kept on. "If we get an organ at school, I can play for everyone. And I can play for Erik when he sings at church."

Josie looked quickly at Kate, but Kate looked away. She couldn't bear to speak one word. Not even with Josie.

Without looking back, Kate hurried off. Pushing open the heavy church door, she ran down the steps. All the way home she sat between Erik and Anders, filled with misery.

———

That afternoon Kate moved restlessly from window to window. Near the dining room, the branches of a tall pine reached out to the house. In the winter sunlight its blue-gray shadows stretched long across the snow.

Finally Kate sat down at her reed organ. Starting with her favorite hymns, she began to play. As the music spoke to her, she played on and on. *It doesn't matter what Maybelle says*, Kate finally told herself. *What matters is that I practice and do the best I can.*

A short time later, Mama lit the kerosene lamp. "Better get the milking done, Kate."

Anders' ankle was swollen again, and he sat with his leg stretched across a chair. Mama wanted him to keep it there.

Slowly Kate stood up. Here the kerosene light spread a soft

glow. Near the wood stove, the room felt warm and cozy. But Kate knew from the draft along the walls how cold it would be outside—and how dark.

In the kitchen she pulled overalls over her dress and long stockings. Anders called after her. "Don't forget the water heater, Kate."

Lars followed Kate to the kitchen. The tuft of hair stood up at the back of his red head. "Mama says I'm good enough to help."

Kate grinned. "You're good enough all right."

Under his freckles Lars flushed. "You know what I mean."

"But send him in if he gets chilled," Mama called after Kate.

As Kate opened the outside door, the wind snatched her scarf, blowing the long ends into her face. Winding the scarf around her neck, she hurried to the barn.

Before long, Lars started shivering, and Kate sent him back to the house. Even without his help, the milking went better. Each time Kate filled her bucket, she poured it into a covered pail.

When she finished the cows, she opened the bin of oats. Taking out a scoop, she fed Wildfire. Carefully she closed the cover and locked it. At last she was done.

Picking up one pail and the farm lantern, Kate kicked open the door of the barn. The wind flung it back against the wall. Setting down the lantern and milk, Kate grabbed the door and closed it.

As she twisted the small piece of wood that kept the door shut, Kate glanced toward the side of the log barn. Along the wall it seemed darker than elsewhere. Kate stared, wondering if something was there.

After a long moment, she picked up the lantern. Her boots squeaked on the cold snow as she scurried over to the watering tank.

At the pile of wood she picked up a small chunk. Yet Kate felt strange. Creepy. As if the hair stood up on the back of her neck. As if someone was watching her.

Dropping the wood, Kate listened. *Did I hear something? Did somebody move? Or a boot crunch on the packed snow?*

Kate whirled. Yet she saw nothing beyond the small glow of the lantern. Picking it up, Kate held out the lantern and started back to the pail of milk. As she looked that way, a shadow darker than the others moved against the barn.

Kate's heart leaped into her throat. Her hands trembled. The light of the lantern wavered.

She tried to push away her scared feelings, tried to stop shaking. The few steps to the pail of milk seemed miles long. *Can I leave the pail behind?* she wondered.

Then Kate thought of what Anders would say. *I can't go in without it.* And there were other pails in the barn.

For a long moment Kate stared at the shadows, and they did not move. At last she told herself, *I imagined it. There's nothing there.*

Step by slow step, Kate started toward the milk. She had almost reached the pail when one shadow separated from the rest.

15

Discovery!

The shadow was slender and taller than Kate. Seeming to glide along the side of the barn, it slipped around the corner.

Forgetting the milk, Kate turned and ran. But she felt as if she were living a nightmare. Her legs felt spongy, as though she could not move. The path from the barn to the house took forever.

Tumbling into the kitchen, Kate slammed the door behind her. Leaning back against it, she tried to catch her breath.

Anders looked up from the kitchen table. "A bandit got you, Kate?"

Kate shook her head, her eyes wide. She drew a long, ragged breath.

"Oh, c'mon now. Something must have scared you."

Kate nodded her head up and down, but still could not speak. As she tried to point outside, her hand trembled.

Anders stood up. "Well, I'm sure whatever it was is only in your imagination."

Kate found her voice. "See for yourself!"

"I will." Gathering up his crutches, Anders swung over to the door. Pulling on his coat, he went outside.

Kate followed slowly, wanting only to stay in the kitchen where the kerosene lamp shed a warm, soft glow. The yard was dark and cold.

But Anders called to her. "Where was it?"

"Over there." Kate pointed toward the side of the barn. "Along that wall."

Anders swung off down the path, heading for the lantern Kate had dropped in the snow. He held it high, but its light barely pierced the darkness.

"What'd you see, Kate?"

"A shadow." Again she pointed.

Anders snorted. "Right. A shadow."

But Kate wasn't going to be put off. "A shadow that moved. It slid around the corner of the barn."

Giving Kate the lantern, Anders swung off on crutches again. "If that's so, there should be footprints in the snow."

"You'll find them all right."

As they reached the barn, she held out the lantern. But there, along the log wall, one footprint crisscrossed another, blurring the shapes.

Lutfisk had been there and some small animals, as well as humans. In the place where Kate had seen the shadow, it was impossible to pick one print from another.

"Look around the end," suggested Kate, "Near the wagon track."

There it was no better. "Can't tell a thing," said Anders, shaking his head. "Too many footprints."

"But there *was* someone there!" Kate protested. "I *know*. I'm sure of it!"

"I'm sure you're just seeing things!"

Kate fell silent. She had to admit she did have a big imagination. But the more she thought about the shadow, the more uneasy she felt. The certainty that there had been something real creeping around the barn wouldn't go away.

———

As Kate pulled on her coat the next morning, Anders came in from outside. His shock of blond hair straggled out from under his cap. "Kate, you let the fire in the tank go out."

In that moment she remembered. She'd started to put in wood, then been scared away. Later, she'd forgotten to go back.

"The tank is a solid hunk of ice," Anders said. "There's not one drop of water for the animals. You're going to have to carry it from the pump. I can't."

Kate groaned, but knew she had no choice. Anders couldn't handle both crutches and a bucket of water.

As she finished watering the cows, Kate stopped near Wildfire's stall. In the sunlight of a nearby window, the mare's coat was brushed smooth. Her black side looked sleek and shiny.

Kate reached up, patting Wildfire's shoulder. As the mare turned to her, Kate stroked the white star in the middle of the black forehead.

When Kate walked around to the mare's other side, she noticed something. Here, too, Wildfire's shoulder looked brushed and smooth. The center of her back seemed just as well groomed. But then the brushing stopped.

On the mare's belly Kate saw the clear line of a cinch strap. There Wildfire's hair lay matted, twisted this way and that. It must have dried wet, without being brushed out.

Kate felt uneasy. She knew she had to tell Anders, but wasn't prepared for what he'd say.

"What did you do, take her out in the middle of the night?" he asked. "After I trusted you to treat her right?"

Kate stared at him. "Are you serious? You know I wouldn't do that."

Anders laughed, but the sound was hard as ice. "You brushed Wildfire, thinking I wouldn't find out. What'd you do, forget the rest? Forget she'd get sick if she's not taken care of?"

Kate felt the hot flush of embarrassment creep into her face. "I promise you. I have not been near your horse since you taught me to ride."

Just then Wildfire sneezed.

"See? I told you!" cried Anders. "She's getting a cold!"

Anders was right. The mare's nose was running.

In spite of being scared, Kate tried to speak quietly. "I didn't do it, Anders. Why would I tell you how she looked if I had taken her out? I could have just brushed her smooth."

"Kate, there hasn't been anyone else around."

"Hasn't there?" Kate's voice was soft, but it had a dangerous edge. "Really now, Anders, hasn't there been anyone else around?"

"What're you talking about?" he asked.

"About last night when you wouldn't believe me."

"Kate, there was nothing there."

"Of course not. By the time you got outside, someone could have easily hidden." Kate picked up a pail and stalked off. Taking a three-legged stool, she sat down and started milking.

Yet the awful feeling that Anders didn't trust her wouldn't go away. Down at the pit of her stomach, Kate felt hurt. *How can I make Anders believe me?* The rest of the morning Kate thought about it, wondering what to do.

Just as often she thought about Mr. Swenson's inheritance. She and Anders needed to get to Josie's and search for the diamond and ruby ring. Time was passing quickly. In just eleven days Swensons would have to move. Yet Anders couldn't possibly go that far on crutches.

The next morning Anders looked even more upset. He and Kate were out in the barn again.

"Wildfire has a cough!" Anders groaned as he checked the mare.

When Anders walked the mare around inside the barn, he noticed something else. "She's limping. She favors one foot."

Turning around from where she milked Clover, Kate watched Anders. She felt scared, so scared she could barely breathe. Her fingers tightened, squeezing harder than she should. Clover stepped sideways.

Kate patted her side. "It's okay, girl. Didn't mean to hurt you."

Standing up, Kate poured the milk into a covered pail and went over to Wildfire.

"See?" said Anders. "She favors her right front foot." He hobbled over to the box that held tools used in the barn. There he found a hoof knife—a straight blade with a curve on the end.

Going back to Wildfire, Anders lifted her front foot and scraped away the mud. Carefully he inspected the hoof.

When he found nothing wrong, Kate left him and fed the sheep. Yet today they offered no comfort.

"Gotta get you over that cold," said Anders to Wildfire.

As though understanding his words, Wildfire coughed. Her nose ran.

"See what I told you?" Again Anders looked worried. "That's what a horse gets if she's ridden hard in cold weather."

Kate started out of the barn, carrying a covered pail of milk in each hand. No matter what she said to Anders, he wouldn't believe her.

As she headed for the house, Anders followed, swinging along on his crutches. "I think I remember everything Papa told me. About taking care of a horse with a cough. About what foundering looks like. But I wish I could make sure."

Kate kept walking. The pails were heavy. Then she had an idea. "Why don't you talk to Mr. Swenson?"

Anders looked thoughtful. "Yup. That's what I should do. But I don't have a way to get there. What we need is one of those newfangled telephones."

Near the house, Kate stopped in the path and swung around. "I could take you."

"*You* take *me*?"

"Pull you on the sled."

The sled was large and used for hauling wood. In spite of his height Anders could easily fit on it. Yet the minute Kate spoke, she wondered if she'd be sorry. A blacksmith had put iron on the bottom of the wooden runners to help the sled glide. Even so, it'd be hard work getting Anders all the way to Swensons.

When they talked to Mama, she said, "Lars can help you, Kate. He's better today."

It was well past lunch before they got started. The weather was mild for January, and the air felt warm on Kate's cheeks. She breathed deeply, grateful to be outdoors.

Lars also looked happy to be out in the sun.

Swinging forward on his crutches, Anders dropped down on the large sled. It had four posts, one at each corner, to hold split wood in place. Settling himself between the posts, Anders angled his crutches across his lap. Kate and Lars took up the rope.

The sled pulled easily on the icy track that passed the barn, then the farmhouse. Often people came this way, taking the shortcut through the woods.

At the top of the hill overlooking Rice Lake there was more snow. There Kate spotted Wildfire's hoof prints on the trail to Spirit Lake School. When Kate pointed them out to Anders, he looked thoughtful but said nothing.

Throwing the rope onto the sled, Kate and Lars gave it a good push. Anders hung on as the sled swooped down the steep track. Kate and Lars followed, then stopped. Near the bottom of the hill, they saw Wildfire's hoofprints again. It looked as if the mare had stopped to drink at the spring.

Soon Kate and Lars caught up to Anders and once again pulled the sled. Farther on, the wind across Rice Lake had blown across the path, sweeping it clean. Patches of dirt and small stones showed through the snow.

For a time they lost Wildfire's hoof prints. Then Anders called out, "Stop!"

Using his crutches, Anders pulled himself up and off the sled. Being careful where he stepped, he studied the ground. At last he pointed down.

"What is it?" asked Kate.

"See the marks in the snow? Something scared Wildfire. She stopped suddenly. Her front feet dug into the dirt."

"Why would she stop right here?" Kate wanted to know.

Anders shrugged. "Maybe a grouse flew up. Or a small animal ran out right in front of her."

He started back to the sled, but Kate had another question. "Could something happen to a horse if it stopped too fast?"

"Too fast?" Anders started to laugh. Then the grin disappeared from his face. Hobbling back, he studied the hoof prints. "You might be right, Kate," he said at last. "I'll check when I get back."

16

The Loan Shark Returns

*M*aybe *Anders will believe me now,* thought Kate as they went on. *Maybe he'll find out what's really wrong with Wildfire.* The idea filled her with hope.

Beyond Rice Lake, they entered the woods and soon came to a fork in the trail. In the open area the wind had blown large drifts across the path.

Kate groaned. If she went ahead, she'd be into snow far above her knees. For Lars it would be even worse.

Anders stopped them. "Why don't you go left on the path to Erik's. It's usually not as drifted. If he's home, he'll help you pull the rest of the way."

By the time they reached Lundgrens', it was midafternoon. Erik went on with them, while Lars returned to Windy Hill Farm.

"Let's take the road past school," Erik suggested. "Sleighs have been through, packing a trail."

As they rounded the bend beyond Spirit Lake School, Kate saw Maybelle ahead. Kate slowed her steps, but it was too late. Maybelle waited until they caught up.

"Going to Josie's?" Anders asked.

Maybelle held up a pair of ice skates. "Grandfather gave me these. He told me to ask Mr. Swenson to weld them where they're broken."

When they reached Josie's farm, Maybelle dropped her skates on the packed snow near the blacksmith shop.

"Don't you want to put 'em in the shop?" asked Anders.

"Mr. Swenson will find them," Maybelle said carelessly and followed the others to the house.

Josie met them at the door. "You're just the ones I wanted to see!" Her eyes danced, and Kate wondered what had happened.

Holding Calico in her arms, three-year-old Becca peeked out from behind her big sister. The little girl's light brown hair curled softly around her face. She smiled, and her hazel eyes sparkled like Josie's.

The aroma of baking cookies filled the large kitchen. A number of them were cooling on the table.

"I've got something to tell you," said Josie, a grin from ear to ear. "This morning I found the ring!"

"You *found* it?" Kate couldn't believe the good news. "Where?"

Josie led them into the large open room. She pointed to a chair. "Right there. When I cleaned, it was near one of the legs. So close that I almost missed it."

"That's strange," said Kate. "We looked there. I know we did. How could the ring suddenly appear when it's been missing for two weeks?"

"I don't know," answered Josie. "We can't even guess how long it's been there. All we know is that it's back!"

"Where's the ring now?" asked Anders. "Can we see it?"

Josie shook her head. "Sorry. I wish I could show you. But Papa hid it in a really good place. We watched him put it away and promised we wouldn't tell anyone."

"All of you saw where he put it?" asked Anders. "Even Stretch?"

"Anders!" Kate warned.

But Josie had already heard. "You think he stole it, then put it out again, don't you?"

"Well—"

"Well, nothing!" snapped Josie, sparks in her hazel eyes. "Quit putting the blame on him!"

Anders said no more. Just the same, Kate could see he was thinking. She had to admit the whole thing seemed mighty strange.

It was strange, too, that Maybelle stood so quietly, listening intently to everything they talked about.

But Josie led them back to the kitchen. "Let's have cookies to celebrate finding the ring."

As everyone sat down at the table, Anders looked at Erik, and Erik looked at Anders. Kate recognized it as their old signal. She'd seen them talk that way at Spirit Lake School.

When Josie poured milk, Erik spoke up. "Josie, does your father have any explanation?"

Josie shook her head. "And neither does Mama. They just say, 'It was gone, and now it's back.' "

"But what if it disappears again?" asked Erik, his eyes troubled.

"It won't," replied Josie. "Tomorrow morning Papa will take the ring to Minneapolis. He'll find an honest man and sell it."

"Your father's leaving tomorrow?" Erik looked relieved.

"First thing in the morning," said Josie. "Papa will drive the team to Grantsburg and take the Blueberry Special." The train took passengers to Rush City where they transferred to another train bound for Minneapolis.

"You'll be able to pay that loan shark off?" asked Anders.

"Papa hopes he can pay off the whole farm. Plus buy machinery he needs. And tools." Josie's eyes glowed. "Papa won't know how to act. He and Mama have always struggled to make payments."

Erik knew all about that. "It's hard enough when payments are fair. But yours are way too high."

"Until now," said Kate, trying to comfort Josie. She knew the long hours Mr. Swenson worked.

"Until tomorrow." Josie smiled as she passed the cookies. "Can you imagine what it'll be like to own the farm, free and clear?"

"Hooray!" said Becca, and all of them laughed.

Becca held Josie's kitten up to Kate. "Pretty kitty."

Kate reached out to take Calico. In that instant the kitten leaped from Becca's hands. Like a shot, Calico streaked into the other room. By the time Kate reached the doorway, the kitten had disappeared.

"She's gone again!" Kate exclaimed as Josie and Erik followed her into the large open room. "Where can she be?"

Josie shrugged. "I'd certainly like to know. She has to be somewhere in the house."

"Somewhere in this room, you mean," answered Kate. "Isn't this where she always disappears?"

"Always," answered Josie.

"Let's search again," said Kate, unwilling to let a mystery go unsolved. "Let's look in every corner of the room."

"There are only four corners, Kate," said Anders as he hobbled in from the kitchen. "You look while I talk to Mr. Swenson about Wildfire. Where's your father, Josie?"

"In the barn, I think. That's where Mama and the boys are."

As Anders and Erik left, Maybelle called after them. "Tell Mr. Swenson I left skates for him to fix."

Josie returned to baking cookies. Maybelle dropped into a chair. Her deep brown eyes looked amused that Kate searched so hard.

Starting on one side of the large room, Kate worked her way around it. As before, she peered behind the large heating stove, inside the wood box, and under the large oak table and chairs.

As last she reached the wall next to the kitchen. Between the door and the chimney, shelves stretched from above Kate's head to close to the floor.

Seeming eager to help, Becca pulled a chair away from the large oak table. She dragged it over next to Kate and climbed up. Standing on the chair, Becca put one foot on a shelf, grabbed the edge of the shelf above and pulled herself up. As she reached for the shelf beyond that, Kate stopped her.

"Josie, come see your sister," Kate called into the kitchen.

Josie took Becca down. "Mama says she's much more of a climber than I was. She's like the boys." She turned to Becca.

"Don't do that again. You'll get hurt."

Kate went back to her search, but Becca acted restless. "Out?" she asked Josie.

"You can find Mama," Josie told her and helped the little girl put on her coat and scarf. As Becca started across the yard, Josie watched from a window.

Kate went back to the shelves. From the chair where she sat, Maybelle still looked amused at Kate's search. But then they heard a cry from outside.

"Becca fell!" exclaimed Josie. "Near the shop."

She and Kate grabbed their coats. Outside, they saw Stretch run from the blacksmith shop, pick up Becca, and start toward the house. As Josie and Kate hurried to meet them, Becca wailed.

Awkwardly Stretch patted her back, trying to comfort her.

As Josie reached them, she held out her arms to Becca. The little girl shook her head and clung to Stretch. But she continued to scream.

"Shhhhh," he soothed. "You'll be all right."

Becca's wails changed to long sobbing whimpers.

Coming into the kitchen, Stretch set Becca down on the table. He stepped back, and Kate saw the blood on his shirt. In spite of the cold, he hadn't waited to put on a coat.

Then Kate saw Becca's knee. Her stocking and the long underwear beneath were ripped and stained with blood.

Gently Josie pulled the torn cloth away from the ugly gash. Blood dripped down Becca's leg.

Kate's eyes blurred with tears. The little girl had taken a hard tumble. The wound was deep and still bleeding. Whatever Becca had fallen on must have been sharp.

Josie hurried to the pail of drinking water near the door. Ladling water into a bowl, she wet a clean cloth.

Kate reached forward to grasp Becca's hands. "Josie's going to help you," she said.

Carefully Josie wiped the area around the gash. Becca wailed. Frantically she tried to push Josie away. But Kate held Becca's hands firm.

Quick tears came to Josie's eyes. "Sorry, Becca," she said. "I don't like this either." Taking a clean cloth, she pressed it against the wound.

Becca screamed.

The wail pierced Kate's heart. "It's all right, Becca," she soothed. "You'll feel better soon."

"Just let me fix it," said Josie. The tears spilled over and ran down her cheeks. With her free hand she pushed the hair out of her sister's eyes.

After a minute Josie let up on the cloth. Immediately the bleeding started again.

"You have to hold it longer," said Stretch.

Taking another cloth, Josie pressed it against Becca's knee. Again the three-year-old screamed.

Stretch's arm tightened around her shoulders. "Shush!" he told her. "Yelling isn't going to make it any better."

In the middle of the wail, Becca stopped. She drew a deep shuddering breath. "You mad, Stretch?"

"Nope, I'm not mad. Just want to help you. Like Josie and Kate."

Once more Josie placed a clean cloth against the wound. Becca flinched, and Kate tightened her grip on the little girl's hands. But this time Becca understood they wanted to help.

"What happened?" Kate asked.

"She fell on some skates," Stretch growled. "They're mighty sharp for a little girl."

Josie's eyes widened. "What do you mean?"

"They were lying on the ground outside the shop. You know the part that has clamps for holding the skate on a shoe? That narrow edge?"

Kate glanced toward Maybelle. Lying on its side, that narrow edge would be sharp as a knife.

Josie's eyes flashed with anger. "Who left skates where Becca could fall on them?"

Kate knew. Turning to Maybelle again, she waited.

Maybelle flushed red. Looking away, she avoided Kate's eyes. As Kate stared at her, the silence in the kitchen grew long.

At last Maybelle spoke. "I did," she said slowly. "But why did Becca have to be so clumsy and fall on them?"

Josie gasped. Becca's bottom lip quivered.

Stretch glared at Maybelle. "Big help *you* are."

Maybelle reached for her coat. "Grandpa wants Mr. Swenson to weld the skates," she said stiffly. Without saying she was sorry, she went out the door.

When Becca's knee stopped bleeding, Josie pressed yet another cloth against the wound. Then Kate wrapped the knee with a long strip torn from an old sheet.

By now Becca was sleepy from crying. Taking the little girl in her arms, Josie sat down in the large rocker in a corner of the kitchen. As Josie rocked back and forth, Becca clutched her favorite blanket and looked up at Stretch.

The tall blond boy leaned forward. "Wish I had a little sister like you," he said.

Becca held out her blanket, and Stretch grinned. "Thanks, Becca. But you better keep it for now."

As Josie rocked her, Becca's long lashes rested on her cheek. Drowsily she opened her eyes, then closed them in sleep.

A moment later sleigh bells jingled in the yard. Through the window Kate saw a pair of matched grays pulling a cutter. The horses seemed familiar. So did the man who drove them.

"Uh-oh," she said. "That man is back."

"Mr. Harris?" Josie spoke softly. Trying to not wake Becca, she pushed her foot against the wood floor and turned the chair toward the window. "It's him all right."

As Mr. Harris tied the grays to the rail, he looked around. Below the thick mustache a satisfied smile crossed his face.

"So he thinks it's his already," said Josie. "Well, we'll show *him!*"

"I'll find your parents," said Stretch and hurried out the back way.

Mr. Harris headed toward the house, his step light and quick. Today a cane hung over his arm, but Kate felt sure he didn't need it for walking. His sealskin cap rested at a jaunty angle on his forehead. His long raccoon coat swung open.

A moment later Mr. Harris knocked on the front door.

17

Frightening News

$\mathcal{T}$hat awful man!" Trying not to wake Becca, Josie whispered. Yet Kate caught a fighting spirit in her friend's voice.

"I'll get the door," Kate said.

"No, just wait," answered Josie. "Give Mama and Papa more time to get here."

Once more Mr. Harris knocked on the door. His pounding seemed to shake the house.

Kate stood up, but Josie put her hand on Kate's arm, telling her again to wait.

In spite of the noise, Kate grinned. "You're stubborn, aren't you?"

Josie grinned back. "I'm stubborn all right. I've seen what he does to Mama and Papa."

Then in the fading light of the short winter day they saw Mr. Swenson start from the barn. "All right," whispered Josie. "Open the door."

By now it sounded as if Mr. Harris would break through the wood. Kate grasped the handle and yanked the door open.

Caught off balance, Mr. Harris almost fell in. He blinked, then recovered. "I don't believe I know you," he said stiffly. "Tell

Mr. Swenson that Mr. Leonard Harris is here."

Kate swung the door wide, and the man entered. Taking off his long coat, Mr. Harris handed it to Kate, along with his cane and sealskin cap.

Mr. Harris looked around the room, again appearing to like what he saw. Choosing the best chair, he sat down.

A moment later an out-of-breath Mr. Swenson entered the room. Smoothing back her hair, Mrs. Swenson followed.

This time Mr. Swenson did not close the door. From the kitchen Kate and Josie heard every word.

"I came to remind you again about the money," Mr. Harris said. "Your payment is due on January twenty-fifth. I won't wait any longer."

Through the doorway Kate saw Mr. Swenson straighten his shoulders. His large hands clenched and unclenched. "You won't have to. I'll have the money for you."

"You've said that before."

"And I've had the money before."

"But where *is* this money you're talking about? I have to have the full amount. And I don't see it."

"You will. I'm a man of my word."

"And I too," said Mr. Harris. His chest seemed to expand. "In exactly ten days you'll be out of this house. But I'm not a coldhearted man. If you don't want your family in the snow, find another place for them!"

Mr. Swenson drew himself up to his full height. "My family will live here. This is my farm, and it will stay that way."

Mr. Harris laughed. Standing up, he walked close to Josie's father.

Mr. Swenson held his ground. "I have an inheritance." He spoke quietly, but reminded Kate of an oak rooted deep. "Tomorrow I will sell a ring my father gave me. You'll have the money in time. The full amount. I give you my word."

Mr. Harris stepped back. "I don't believe you. Don't forget, you have only ten days." Calling for his coat, he stalked out of the house.

A minute later, Mr. Harris climbed into his cutter. Through the kitchen window, Kate saw his long whip snake out. The grays leaped ahead. Then the growing dusk closed around them.

Slowly Josie stood up with Becca still in her arms. "I'm glad she didn't hear," said Josie, looking down at her sleeping sister. "And I'm glad my brothers were outside."

The Swensons had known other hard times, but Kate had never seen Josie so upset. Tears slid down her white cheeks.

When Kate and Josie went into the other room, Mrs. Swenson stood in front of a window. Her fingers nervously twisted her apron. Staring at the spot where Mr. Harris was last seen, Mrs. Swenson talked to herself.

"What's she saying?" Kate whispered to Josie.

"Her favorite verse. Whenever Mr. Harris comes, Mama gets so worried she repeats it over and over."

Kate strained to hear.

"Casting all your care upon him," Mrs. Swenson muttered, still staring out the window. "Casting all your care upon him, for he careth for you."

"That's Mama's verse!" Kate cried.

Mr. Swenson turned away from the door. He no longer looked the bold man who had stood up to Mr. Harris. "Yah, the Lord cares for us," he said. "Our good Lord had my father send the ring just in time!"

Shortly after, Kate, Erik, and Anders left for home. As they walked, Kate thought of only one thing. *What would Swensons do if they didn't have the ring?*

Soon the three of them passed Spirit Lake School, then the Lundgren house. Erik stayed with them, helping Kate pull Anders on the sled.

By the time they entered the woods between Erik's house and Windy Hill Farm, the moon shone high and clear. Its glow brightened the snow and lit a path through the woods. The trees cast shadows that lengthened with the night.

Kate shivered and wished they were home, warm and cozy around the wood stove. As a sound shattered the night air, Kate jumped.

"It's just an owl," Anders called out from the sled. "Stop acting like a girl."

"I *am* one!" Kate responded. "And proud of it!"

"But he's right, Kate," Erik said, his voice low, as though not wanting to embarrass her in front of Anders. "You don't have to be scared. Listen."

The call came again, and Kate heard it distinctly. *Whoo, whoo, whoo, whoo—whoo, whoo, whoo, whoo-ah!*

Taking a deep breath, Kate tugged on the rope and trudged ahead. Yet every sound tightened her nerves.

Close at hand, a branch cracked, sounding like a pistol shot. Again Kate jumped, and Anders laughed.

"What a scaredy-cat!"

"I am *not*!" Kate answered. "You know I'm not!"

"Don't know nothin'!" Anders told her. "Just watching how you act."

From then on Kate stared straight ahead, barely moving her head. Yet always she watched, her eyes trying to pierce the shadows on either side of the path.

As they moved onto the open field between the two houses, Kate saw a dark shape on the path ahead. Moving quickly, it rushed toward them.

Kate shrieked, but Anders laughed. "See what I mean? You're a scaredy-cat!"

Then Kate saw it was Lutfisk. The dog leaped toward the sled, licked Anders' face, and woofed. Grateful that it wasn't a wild animal, Kate tried to shrug away her fear.

As soon as they reached Windy Hill Farm, Anders headed straight for the barn. Kate and Erik followed him.

Erik lit a lantern, and Anders found the hoof knife he used before. Leading Wildfire to the light, Anders lifted the mare's right front foot. Carefully he scraped away the dirt.

Erik held the lantern close. The outer part of Wildfire's hoof looked like a tough fingernail. Suddenly Anders stopped his cleaning.

"That's it!" he exclaimed.

Leaning forward, Kate saw what looked like a small dark circle near the outer edge of the hoof. As Anders worked with the knife, a sharp little pebble popped out.

"There it is!" Anders looked relieved.

"That's what made Wildfire limp?" Kate asked.

"I think so." Anders let down the mare's foot and patted her shoulder. "Now you're going to feel better, girl."

"How'd you know to look for a stone?" asked Kate.

Anders pushed the blond hair out of his eyes. "Remember that place on the trail? Where you asked if something could happen to a horse if it stopped too fast? I thought something might have jumped out and scared Wildfire. She stopped so suddenly her hooves ground through the snow into the dirt."

"And she picked up a stone?" Kate felt good. For the first time since Anders found the oat bin open, the air seemed clear between them. "Will Wildfire be all right now?" she asked.

"I don't know. We'll have to see." Anders looked Kate straight in the eye. "That's why you need to check a horse's hooves after taking 'em out."

His voice sounded sharp, and Kate's hope vanished like smoke in the wind. Anders still suspected her.

Kate ached with disappointment. "I told you. I didn't take Wildfire out."

"Then who did?"

Kate saw the unbelief in his eyes. *If my own brother doesn't trust me, who will?* she asked herself. It didn't matter that Anders was only a stepbrother. They'd known each other almost nine months.

Kate's disappointment turned to pain. Lifting her head, she tossed her black braid over her shoulder. *Anders will never believe me. Not until I find out who took Wildfire from the barn.*

Then Kate had an idea. *Maybe Stretch would understand how I feel. Maybe he can tell me what to do.*

A few days later Anders sat in the kitchen, a newspaper spread out on the table before him. He read from the January eighteenth *Journal of Burnett County.*

"Look at this!" Anders whistled.

Standing behind him, Kate read over her brother's shoulder. In a bold headline the paper said: BOUNTY PAID FOR WILD ANIMALS BY BURNETT COUNTY IN 1906.

"Bounty? What's a bounty?" Kate asked, forgetting for a moment the unsettled feelings between her and Anders.

"A reward," he told her. "See? Right along the top here." He pointed to small type at the top of four columns.

To Whom Paid was the first column, and under it a list of names. Next came *Amount* and the dollars paid out. Then *Kind of Animal*.

Kate read down the list. "One wolf, two wild cats, one lynx, fourteen wolves." She paused at the awfulness of it. "*Fourteen* wolves?"

"Yup." Anders didn't seem very disturbed. He pointed farther down. "Usually it's not that many. But eight, nine, three. Oh, here's another fourteen."

"Where?" Kate asked, barely able to whisper. "Where were they killed?"

Then she saw the fourth column and picked out the places closest to Windy Hill Farm. "Grantsburg, Wood Lake, Trade Lake."

In that instant Anders looked up at her face. "Do you know why there's a bounty?" he asked.

Kate shook her head.

"Because wild animals kill *our* animals."

But Kate still could not speak.

"What's scaring you?" Anders asked.

When Kate finally answered, her lips felt stiff. "I hear the wolves at night."

Anders grinned, but for once did not tease. Kate wondered if he remembered the promise he had made when Papa said, "Take care of Mama and Kate."

"They won't bother you, Kate. You're safe inside the house."

"But what *will* they bother?" she asked. Deep inside, Kate's scared feeling wouldn't go away.

"Animals that are sick and old," Anders told Kate. "Ones that can't run fast anymore. And wolves bother sheep and calves. They're pretty helpless, you know."

When Anders put away the newspaper, Kate was glad. She didn't want to think about the wolves. "That's why you always get the sheep in before dark."

It wasn't a question. Kate knew the answer.

18

Growing Threats

*E*arly the next morning Erik pounded on the Windy Hill door. "Josie's brother just came to our place," Erik said. "The ring is gone!"

"Missing?" Kate couldn't believe it. "I thought Mr. Swenson sold it right after we were there. Didn't he go to Minneapolis?"

Erik shook his head. "The day he was supposed to go, Josie's youngest brother woke up awfully sick. Mr. Swenson had to go for the doctor and never made it to Minneapolis."

A hard knot formed at the pit of Kate's stomach. "The ring is *really* gone again?"

Erik's blue eyes darkened with anger. "It's *really* gone. Josie wants all of us to come and help them look. This time we're going over the entire farm with a fine-tooth comb."

Erik helped Kate and Anders with chores. While Kate finished up, Erik carried pails of milk into the house. Anders hobbled after him, also carrying a pail and using one crutch.

When Kate entered the kitchen, the boys sat at the table with Mama. Looking Kate's way, everyone stopped talking. The next instant they all spoke at once.

It made Kate uncomfortable. *Are they talking about me?* she wondered. She tried to push her feelings aside.

Soon after, she and Erik and Anders started out, with Anders again on the sled. After a time he walked part of the way, being careful to favor his bad ankle.

When they reached Josie's house, Mr. Swenson sat in the kitchen drinking coffee. His eyes looked bleak, his face lined with worry.

They found Josie in the large open room. "When my brother got better, Papa went to get the ring," she explained. "That's when he discovered it was gone!"

"Could Mr. Harris have come back?" asked Kate. "Could he have stolen the ring?"

"We'd have seen him," said Josie. "We've been here the whole time." Her eyes looked scared. "But this is just what that old loan shark wants! In four days we'll lose the house!"

Four days, thought Kate. *The last time the ring disappeared, it was gone for two weeks. This time it might be gone for good.*

So afraid she could barely think, Kate stared out the window. Only a few days before, Mr. Harris had driven up to that hitching rail. With his handsome cold eyes he looked around as though wanting everything within reach. The idea of that terrible man taking the farm made Kate shiver right down to her toes.

Then she realized something. *This is where Josie's mother stood. She watched that old loan shark. She knew he had the power to take away the farm. She knew he could take even this house— the house where she and Mr. Swenson lived with their nine children.* Again Kate shivered, but not from cold.

Then Kate remembered Mrs. Swenson repeating the verse to herself. When Kate turned back to the room, she no longer felt afraid.

"Did you ask Stretch about the ring?" Anders asked Josie.

"Papa refuses." Josie's eyes were dark with pain. "He says we can trust Stretch."

"But what if you trust him, and he robs you of your farm?" growled Anders.

"Anders, you don't have proof," said Erik. "You're blaming Stretch because of his reputation."

"Right," agreed Anders. "If we trust him, Josie's whole family might get hurt."

"Do you have any clues?" Kate asked Josie.

"Whoever took the ring left the boxes again. They were left open the same way. Do you want to see them?"

Kate picked up the boxes—the small one that held the ring and the slightly larger one for mailing. Going to the window, she held them up.

There in the sunlight she saw something new. "Josie!" Kate cried. "Do you think these are fingerprints?"

One gray smudge marked the larger box. "It's hard to say for sure on this one," Kate replied as Josie looked on. "It might have gotten dirty in the mail. But here's something I didn't see before."

In the light of the window Kate turned the smaller box. "See this fingerprint? It's smudged a bit and isn't clear. But look on the other side of the box. There's another mark just like the first. Both fingerprints are where someone would hold the box to open it."

"You're right, Kate!" Erik sounded excited.

"How big a finger would make that smudge?"

He grinned. "A small one."

Kate felt so relieved that she laughed. "That's what I thought too. All we have to do is figure out who that finger belongs to. Let's look at the hands of everyone we see."

They also decided to search the house, then the other buildings. Josie and Anders went to the granary, while Kate and Erik looked in every part of the barn. After three hours even Kate had to admit they were looking for a needle in a haystack. Finally they had no choice but to give up.

As Erik went to find Josie and Anders, Kate started across the farmyard. There she ran into Stretch. Instead of meeting her gaze, the boy with the blond curly hair looked away.

But Kate remembered her idea and spoke quickly before he could leave. She told Stretch how Anders didn't trust her, then asked, "What should I do?"

"You have to catch whoever's comin' into your barn," Stretch answered promptly.

"But how?" asked Kate, even though she knew he was right.

"Does the rider always come at night?"

Kate nodded. "So far."

"Then hide in your barn," said Stretch. "Wait there 'til you find out who it is. I'd help you if I could, but I gotta stay here."

"Thanks, Stretch," said Kate, feeling better already.

"Be sure you hide where the person won't find you," he warned.

———

When Kate went to her room that night, she stayed fully dressed. Wrapping herself in a warm blanket, she knelt by the window overlooking the wagon track.

When the house grew quiet, Kate tiptoed downstairs, pulled on her heavy coat, scarf, and mittens, and slipped outside. Hurrying to the barn, she climbed up in the hayloft.

Near the large hole into the main floor of the barn, Kate settled deep in the hay. For a long time she waited with eyes wide open. Fighting down her fear of the dark, she peered through the hole into the floor below.

Gradually Kate grew sleepy. When she wakened, she felt cold all the way through.

What time is it? Kate wondered. She had no idea, but guessed it was very late. She knew only that she had to get warm.

As she quietly opened the kitchen door, the clock chimed four times. Tiptoeing, Kate headed toward the wood cookstove. A voice stopped her.

"What were you doing outside?" Anders asked from the doorway to the dining room.

Kate jumped.

"Been out riding my horse?"

From the middle of the kitchen, Kate faced him. "No," she answered, her voice strong in spite of the scare Anders had given her. "I'm trying to discover who *is* riding Wildfire."

Anders looked as if he didn't believe a word she said. "What're you talking about?"

"Sooner or later the person who took your horse will come back. I'm going to be there."

Anders stared at her. "Maybe you're right," he said slowly. "Don't know why I didn't think of it myself. But I know one thing. I don't want you sitting there alone. I'll go with you."

Grabbing his coat, Anders hobbled out on one crutch. As they crossed the yard to the barn, Kate looked up. In the night sky just before dawn, the stars seemed close enough to touch.

Inside the barn Anders pulled himself up the ladder with his strong arms and one foot. Kate handed up his crutch, then followed. Settling down in the dusty hay, she again peered through the hole into the floor below.

Time dragged on, as each minute seemed to last forever. Yet Kate felt glad for Anders' company. It wasn't as frightening waiting together.

In a crack between the boards of the outside wall, Kate watched streaks of pink edge into the eastern sky. Suddenly she caught her breath.

"Shhhh!" warned Anders. "Someone's coming!"

"I have to sneeze!" Quickly Kate covered her nose and mouth with her hands.

"No, no!" whispered Anders. "Shhhhh!"

From below, the latch of the door jiggled. As someone opened, then closed the door, it squeaked on its hinges. Through the hole into the main floor of the barn, Kate saw a shadow quietly move their way.

Again Kate gasped, trying to hold back her sneeze. The next instant it came. "Achoooo!"

The shadow leaped away, bumping into the stall with a loud thump.

When the door slammed, Anders was already partway down the ladder. Kate tumbled after him as Anders hobbled outside. They each took a different direction around the barn. But whoever the person was had gotten away.

"Aw, Kate, how could you?" complained Anders when they met again near the barn door. "How could you possibly sneeze right then?"

In the first light of dawn Kate saw her brother's face and guessed how upset he felt. "I'm sorry, Anders," she said, her voice low. She felt sick with disappointment. "We were mighty close."

"Close, all right! And now he might not try again—not for a while anyway. We would have caught him right in the act."

Him? Kate wondered. "Who do you think it was?" she asked. But Anders only shrugged.

At least he knows there's SOMEONE, thought Kate. Still it gave her little comfort. She looked away, then down, tracing a pattern in the snow with her foot.

Then she saw it. As the sun edged higher in the sky, Kate saw something dark against the snow. Something close to her foot and closer to the door. Reaching down, she picked it up.

A black button!

"Look, Anders!" She held it out for him to see, then turned it over in her hand. "Four holes for thread to pass through. A raised outer ridge."

A lopsided grin lit her brother's face. "Well, we didn't do so bad after all!"

Kate agreed. Carefully she slipped the button deep inside the pocket of her coat.

All through chores she tried to remember where she'd seen such a button. As soon as they finished milking, she and Anders hurried to Erik's, and the three went on to Josie's. Again Anders rode on the sled, but also walked part way, trying to strengthen his injured ankle.

"Only three more days," said Kate, thinking about Swensons. "Today, tomorrow, and Thursday."

"Not even that," Anders corrected her. "On Thursday Mr. Swenson has to go to Minneapolis and sell the ring. Friday morning he's got to come back on the train."

"And pay for the farm," Kate replied, "before they lose it."

Making the deadline for the payment seemed impossible. Kate glanced at Erik. He looked just as worried as Anders.

When they reached Swensons, Josie and Anders searched the chicken coop while Kate and Erik headed for the blacksmith shop. Both of them felt embarrassed about having to look through the shop.

Stretch didn't make it easier. "You won't find anything here," he said bluntly.

"We believe that, Stretch," answered Erik. "We trust you. But we need to look in case someone slipped in when you weren't here."

Stretch seemed to accept Erik's words. As Kate and Erik searched, the tall blond boy shaped a cherry hot piece of iron on the anvil. Yet he pounded halfheartedly, as if he didn't care about his work.

Finally Stretch dropped the iron into a pail of water. He looked at Erik with a strange expression on his face.

"I ain't got nothin' to keep me here," Stretch burst out, as though finishing something he and Erik had talked about before.

"Nothing? That's not true," Kate protested.

She remembered how sure of himself Stretch had seemed when she first met him at Spirit Lake School. Though he was older than the other children, they liked him. They wanted Stretch on their side for games. With his help they'd win.

But now Stretch looked discouraged. "I got nothin' to keep me here," he said again.

"You have a chance to make good," Erik told him. "Mr. Swenson says you could be one of the best blacksmiths around."

"I could be," Stretch agreed, "and I'd like my own shop someday. Maybe in Grantsburg. But it's no use trying."

"Why?" demanded Kate.

"If people don't trust me, I can't get work," Stretch told her. "Even if I got my own shop, they wouldn't come."

"But Mr. Swenson believes in you," Kate answered.

"Don't make no difference," said Stretch. "Other folks don't. Including your brother Anders."

Kate fell silent, knowing Stretch was right.

In a moment the tall thin boy spoke again. "If folks don't trust me, I'm not sticking around."

"What would you do?" she asked.

"I'd leave."

"You'd go home?" Kate wanted to know. "To your family's farm?"

Stretch shook his head. "Nothin' to keep me there either."

"But your father?" Kate asked, though she knew Stretch's father was gone. "Won't he come back? Sooner or later, I mean?"

Stretch shrugged his shoulders, looking at the ground instead of Kate or Erik.

Then Kate guessed what really bothered Stretch. "You figure

he won't come home, don't you?"

The tall boy nodded, still avoiding their eyes.

Kate wondered how strongly Stretch meant what he said. She didn't wonder long.

"I'd run away," Stretch said quietly. His voice changed, sounding like the hammer he used to pound iron. "I'd leave and never come back!"

19

The Shadows Lengthen

*I*n spite of the heat from the forge, Kate shivered. Stretch meant it all right. "Where would you go?"

"Aw, Stretch," Erik broke in, "stop talking like that. Big Gust and Mr. Swenson believe in you. Kate and I believe in you. We all know you want to make good."

Stretch seemed to grow even taller than his more than six feet. "No, you don't." His voice filled with anger. "You're a goody-goody, likin' the sound of your words. You're just waitin' for me to do somethin' wrong."

"No, we're not," answered Erik. "But we're not dumb either."

Stretch's laugh was scornful.

"You have to give folks time," Erik went on. "Prove they can trust you."

"Prove it?" Stretch scoffed. "I have."

Erik shook his head. "You've started," he said, sounding older than his thirteen years. "You haven't finished."

"Finished! Ha! That's a laugh!" Stretch went back to his work.

"What are you, a quitter?" Erik asked.

But Stretch picked up a new piece of iron. With angry blows he started to pound it into shape. When he refused to speak again, Kate and Erik left. Stretch did not look their way.

Returning to the farmhouse, Kate found Josie, Anders, and Mrs. Swenson in the kitchen. Suddenly the room grew quiet. Then, as everyone looked at Kate, they all started talking at once.

Kate felt uncomfortable, as though reliving her first day at Spirit Lake School. Then she'd been left out, afraid and alone. Now Kate tried to push that feeling aside. She remembered the way they'd kept Anders' party a secret.

My birthday's tomorrow, Kate thought. All week she'd watched Mama. Yet Kate had never sensed that her mother was getting ready. Not once did Kate sniff the aroma of a freshly baked cake. With Papa gone and the new baby coming, Mama seemed to have all she could handle.

In the next moment Kate forgot about her big day. She and Erik had to tell Swensons they once again had found nothing.

Josie looked white and desperate. "Only twenty-four hours left to search," she said. "After that, Papa has to go to Minneapolis."

And after that the loan shark comes, thought Kate.

———

The next morning Kate woke to her thirteenth birthday. *Will anyone do something special?* she wondered.

At the breakfast table no one wished Kate happy birthday. "Do you remember what day this is?" she asked.

Tina looked at Kate as though she didn't understand. Lars blew his nose. Anders got up to help himself to another piece of toast. And Mama stood at the cookstove. Still fighting a cold, she seemed to not hear.

Someone should remember, thought Kate, trying to ignore her hurt. *Maybe they need a hint.* "It's a nice January day," she said.

"Oh? You think so?" asked Mama.

"Not very cold. Seems like a special day," answered Kate.

But Mama kept stirring whatever was in her kettle.

"Does this seem like a special day to you?" asked Kate, looking around.

Tina shrugged, her eyes wide. Lars coughed into his napkin. Anders heaped butter on his toast.

Finally Kate gave up. *It's bad enough if the others don't re-*

member. But how can my own mother forget? It had been an awful month for Mama, but just the same—

Then Kate remembered. "This is the last day," she said. "The last day for finding Mr. Swenson's ring." When she thought about Swensons losing their farm, her birthday didn't matter at all.

Anders stood up and walked without a crutch. "I'm going over there now," he said. "I've thought of more places to look."

Near the door, he turned back to Kate. "You'll come after chores, won't you? You can walk faster than me anyway. Maybe you'll catch up."

As Kate hurried out to the barn, Anders set off on the trail now broken by horses, sleighs, and people walking. In the barn Kate went to the sheep pen and sank her fingers deep into their heavy coats. *Baaaa!* they welcomed.

When she patted Clover, Kate realized she and the cow had become friends.

Today Kate hurried through the milking, wanting to spend all the time she could at Josie's. As soon as she finished chores, Kate hurried to her room to change clothes. There she brushed out her hair. Unbraided, it fell down her back, thick and shiny. Gathering it together, Kate tied her hair with a ribbon instead of taking time for braids.

As she went outside, the crisp January air felt good on her cheeks. Kate breathed deeply. In the morning sunlight the snow glistened with thousands of diamonds. The walk through the woods seemed special and wonderful, like a gift prepared for her. Yet one thought stayed with her: *If only we could find the ring.*

When Kate reached Josie's, Mrs. Swenson let her in. For a moment Kate stood there, just inside the kitchen. As she hung her coat on a peg by the door, she felt the warmth of the cookstove. Yet something seemed different. The house sounded too quiet for a family of nine children.

Then Mrs. Swenson smiled, and Becca held out a corn-husk doll. Taking Kate's hand, the little girl led her past the stairs leading upward. When they entered the other room, noise exploded around Kate. "Surprise! Surprise!"

Anders jumped up from behind one chair. Erik and Stretch came from behind another. Josie and Maybelle popped out from under the table, while other children seemed to spill into the room.

Then someone began singing "Happy Birthday." Kate stood on the threshold, feeling as if she were going to cry.

"We did it, huh?" Josie laughed. "We really surprised you!"

Kate laughed with her. "You surprised me, all right!"

Josie grinned. "You're so good at solving mysteries, we were afraid you'd figure out this one!"

Kate looked around the room. For the first time she saw a big chocolate birthday cake on the table. In spite of all that had happened, did Mrs. Swenson bake the cake to help Mama?

Then Kate heard a noise in the kitchen. A moment later Mama and Tina, Lars, and Mrs. Lundgren appeared.

"Mama?" Kate asked, unable to believe what she was seeing.

Mama's smile lit even her eyes. "As soon as you left the house, Mrs. Lundgren gave us a ride. We took the longer road around so you wouldn't see."

Reaching out, Mama hugged Kate. "Happy birthday, little colleen."

Kate blinked. Mama hadn't forgotten. She even remembered Daddy O'Connell's special name. So this was what everyone had been planning!

Soon Anders and Erik started the games. Yet as much as she wanted to have fun, Kate couldn't push aside the scared look in Josie's eyes. *How can they have a party for me right now?* Kate wondered. *If they lose the farm, this is the last time we'll be here.*

Whenever Kate looked toward Mrs. Swenson, the kind woman smiled. Yet Kate felt sure the smile covered worry.

After two games Kate said, "Let's spread out and all of us search again. With this many looking, someone might find the ring."

But when they came back together again, no one had found even one clue. Though she tried to smile, Kate could barely eat her cake.

When the party was over, Maybelle was the first to leave. Kate wasn't sorry. At the same time she felt puzzled. More than that, she hated herself for being suspicious.

While eating, Kate had looked at everyone's hands. Maybelle's were small, but so were the hands of some of the other girls. Were any of them small enough to fit the fingerprints on the box? Kate wasn't sure. But she did know one thing. No one had a coat with the kind of button she'd found.

One by one, the partygoers drifted away. As the outside door swung open, Kate saw Lutfisk sitting on the path, waiting for Anders. Then Mrs. Lundgren took Mama and Lars and Tina home. Soon after, Stretch went outside. Through a window Kate saw him splitting wood.

Mrs. Swenson poked her head through the doorway. "Josie, watch Becca while I go out to the barn. She's drawing on a slate in the kitchen."

Looking absentminded, Josie nodded. "Only a few more hours to find the ring," she said to Kate, Anders, and Erik as they sat in the large open room. "If Papa doesn't sell that ring tomorrow, we lose the farm."

Kate's heart felt as if it were being squeezed. "Let's go over everything that happened," she said. "Maybe we can figure out something we've missed."

"I don't understand how that ring could disappear twice," said Erik. "Especially with such a large family."

Josie agreed. "One of my brothers and sisters is always here."

"And so is Stretch!" Anders declared. "Stretch took the ring."

"No, he *didn't*!" said Kate.

"I'm sure he did!" Anders stood up. It seemed strange seeing him without crutches. "How could it be anyone but Stretch?" he demanded, his voice growing louder.

"I believe in him," said Kate.

"So do I," chimed in Erik. "He's trying to make good."

As Erik spoke, Kate realized the strangeness of it all. She still felt the pain of Anders not trusting her. *Is that how Stretch hurts inside? Is that why he says he'll give up?*

Kate wanted to take his side. "Stretch has changed," she said. "Why do you blame him?"

"If someone's going to take something, he has to have a reason," Anders told her.

"Well?" demanded Kate. "What's his reason?"

Anders thought for a moment. "He wants those things."

"Wants a ring he couldn't wear around here?" asked Kate. "What would he do with it?"

"Sell it," Anders answered promptly.

Kate shook her head. "That's not a good enough reason."

"Kate's right," Erik broke in. "You don't have proof."

"Listen," said Anders. "In order to take something, a person has to have the opportunity. So who's had plenty of opportunity? Stretch!"

Just then Kate caught a movement back of Anders. A movement near the door to the kitchen. What was it?

Kate jumped up and ran to the doorway. Poking her head into the kitchen, she looked around. Becca sat there, drawing on the slate.

Turning back, Kate gazed up the stairs. Nothing there either.

"Spooks got you, Kate?" Anders asked.

Kate shrugged and returned to the large open room. Sitting down on the floor, she leaned back against the shelves next to the kitchen door.

But her uneasiness wouldn't go away. She had seen something. A shadow. That shadow had slipped past the door.

20

Lutfisk Meets Calico

$\mathcal{A}$s Kate thought about the shadow, Anders went back to his idea.

"A person who takes something needs the opportunity," he said. "The person has to be able to do it."

"Right," drawled Erik. "And we all know Stretch had the opportunity. But that doesn't make him guilty."

"What we have to figure out is who else had the opportunity." Kate was thinking out loud.

"So instead of just blaming Stretch, let's remember who was here when the ring disappeared," said Erik. "And who could have made it reappear."

For a time the room was quiet. Finally Kate broke the silence. "I saw the ring the day after we brought the food."

"How many of us were here that day?" asked Erik.

Kate and Erik looked at each other, then at Anders and Josie. "All of us," Kate answered. "Plus Maybelle."

"And Stretch," said Anders.

Erik turned to Kate. "When did you leave the buckle for your ski?"

"That same day," answered Kate.

"So all of us were here," said Erik.

"Plus Maybelle," added Kate, though she felt strangely uneasy.

"And Stretch," said Anders.

"Now when did the ring show up again?" Erik asked Josie.

"We don't really know," she answered. "We just know when I found it next to that chair leg."

"And when it disappeared again," said Erik.

No one needed to ask the question.

"All of us were here then too!" Anders exclaimed.

"Plus Maybelle." Yet Kate's heart felt heavy. Though she didn't like the other girl, Kate didn't want to believe Maybelle would steal something. Especially from Josie's family.

"And don't forget Stretch," Anders reminded them. "He's been here all the time, like Josie and her brothers and sisters."

Just then Kate wondered if she heard a noise on the stairs. She listened, but no sound came.

"It's Stretch, I tell you!" Anders spoke boldly. "I'm sure he's guilty."

Kate looked at Anders, wondering why he felt so ready to blame the tall thin boy. Maybe if her brother had talked with Stretch the way she and Erik had, Anders wouldn't feel that way.

Just then Kate glanced beyond her brother, and caught a quick movement. Jumping up, she hurried to the window. As she looked out, someone darted around the corner of the house.

Running to the kitchen door, Kate flung it open, tore down the steps, and circled the house. It was too late. Whoever had been there was gone.

Lutfisk still waited outside and followed Kate back to the kitchen door. When she reached the top step, Kate turned to him. "Sit, Lutfisk. Stay."

Lutfisk sat, and Kate felt good about his growing willingness to obey her. But as she opened the door, Josie's kitten bounded out from behind the cookstove.

Suddenly a blur of hair tore up the steps. Brushing past Kate, Lutfisk raced into the kitchen.

Calico hissed and fled into the other room. With a "Woof!" Lutfisk streaked after her. Kate followed the dog.

The kitten leaped into Josie's arms, with Lutfisk only a moment behind. The dog circled Josie, then jumped up. Calico sprang to the floor.

Before Josie could grab her, the kitten tore past Anders. Erik reached down, trying to catch her, but Calico darted between his legs. Erik whirled. In that instant the kitten disappeared.

Lutfisk slid to a halt and cocked his head.

Anders stared at him, then started to laugh. "Lose your victim, old boy?"

His tongue hanging out, Lutfisk seemed to listen. Yet he looked as puzzled as Kate felt.

"Where did Calico go?" she asked.

Even Lutfisk seemed confused. Standing in the middle of the floor, he tipped his head from side to side.

Then he lowered his nose to the floor and sniffed. Passing behind Erik, Lutfisk followed Calico's trail across the room. Near the shelves by the kitchen door, the dog dropped to his belly. For a moment he stayed there, his body tense.

Then, resting his mouth on his front paws, Lutfisk wiggled forward. Close to the wall, he pushed his nose into the narrow space beneath the bottom shelf. "Woof!" he barked.

When Anders called him, Lutfisk refused to leave.

"That's strange," said Kate. "Lutfisk always does what you ask."

"Always," said Anders, a frown creasing his forehead. But instead of going to the dog and forcing him to obey, Anders sat down where he could watch Lutfisk. "I can't figure out what's going on."

Kate also watched the dog. A moment later she jumped up. "Do you see what I see?" Kneeling beside Lutfisk, she took hold of his collar and tried to pull him back.

Lutfisk growled.

Kate wasn't going to be put off. "Get him, will you, Anders?"

As Anders dragged Lutfisk aside, Kate flopped down in the dog's place. For the first time she wondered if the dark space between the bottom shelf and the floor was more than a shadow.

Erik dropped down beside her.

Lying on her stomach, Kate slid her hand into the small space.

Reaching as far as she could, Kate felt along the wall. Her fingers found what she thought she'd seen—a small opening just large enough for a kitten. An opening large enough for an adult hand to slide through.

"Here, kitty!" she called. "Here, Calico. Kitty, kitty, kitty!"

When Calico did not appear, Kate turned back. "You call her, Josie."

"Just a minute," said Anders. "I'll hold Lutfisk."

As Anders pulled the dog farther away, Kate saw one beady eye and a small paw appear in the opening.

Josie took Kate's spot and called several times. Calico would not leave her hiding place. Finally Josie moved back.

"She'll come out when she's hungry," said Erik.

Kate wasn't ready to give up. "Where do you suppose that hole goes?"

"Curious Kate!" Anders hooted. "That's what we'll call you!"

The way Anders sounded, he was back to his old self. Though Kate wouldn't admit it, his teasing almost felt good. *Does he trust me again?* she wondered. It had helped to have Anders there when someone entered the barn. But they still didn't know who that person was.

Kate tossed her head. "Awful Anders, you mean!"

Her brother pushed back his shock of blond hair. His lips parted in a lopsided grin. "Yup, we'll call you curious Kate!"

Ignoring Anders, Kate flopped down on her stomach again. Once more, she reached under the bottom shelf. This time she put her hand, then her arm, inside the hole and felt around. On the other side of the wall was a floor.

Scrunching forward, Kate turned her hand palm up. Wiggling her fingers as far as she could go, she felt a small piece of wood along the inside of the wall. About an inch wide, the wood seemed four or five inches long.

"Aha!"

Still reaching upward, Kate moved her fingers across the wood. In its center she felt the head of a nail. The nail gave Kate an idea. Often a twirling piece of wood held a door shut, providing a lock of sorts.

Moving her fingers to the top of one side, Kate pushed on

the wood. Sure enough, the small piece moved. Again Kate pushed.

Several times she tried. But the piece moved no farther. Feeling puzzled, Kate finally sat back.

"What's there?" asked Erik.

"A piece of wood. It twists on a nail like something to keep a door closed. It moved a little, but it's stuck."

"Let me try," he offered.

Getting down on his stomach, Erik reached inside the hole as Kate had done. Kate stood back, watching. As Erik's arm moved, she knew he was pushing down on the wood. In that instant a shelf in front of Kate quivered.

"Hey! You did something!" she exclaimed.

Erik glanced up. "Did that shelf move, or am I imagining things?"

"It moved all right!" Anders told him. "Maybe the shelves are nailed to a door!"

"Maybe," said Erik. "But if you're right, the door's been closed a long time."

His arm muscles tensed as he pressed again on the small piece of wood. "Here we go!"

Slowly the shelves swung forward into the room.

21

Footsteps Through the Snow

"$\mathscr{I}$t is a door!" Kate yelped.

While she and Anders took hold of the shelves, Erik gripped the hand hold at the bottom and kept pulling.

Creee-e-e-a-a-k! The door squeaked loudly as though long unused. When it stood open as far as it could go, Erik jumped up. All of them peered into the darkness behind the shelves.

Claws clicked against the wood floor. A ball of fur jumped out. Calico leaped into Josie's arms.

Lutfisk barked. Anders grabbed the dog's collar and held him until he settled down. As Anders let go again, Lutfisk sniffed his way into the yawning hole.

"He's showing us where to go!" exclaimed Josie.

Lighting a candle, Kate set it in a holder and brought the small flame to the entrance. Holding out the candle, she stepped into the darkness.

Anders followed close behind, peering over Kate's shoulder. Erik and Josie crowded in.

"Look at that!" Josie pointed to the huge timbers at either side of the entrance.

"We're going through a log wall," said Anders. "Maybe it was a window, and someone changed it to a door."

Kate saw what he meant. The wall was almost a foot deep, the same width as the doorway leading into the kitchen.

Inside the secret space Kate turned around. The room was narrow, probably three feet wide at most. But it was also long, extending from near the kitchen door, behind the chimney, and over to the logs of the outside wall.

On the side opposite the shelf-door, the wall was built of wide, upright boards. Those boards looked new and unweathered when compared with the logs.

Holding up the candle, Kate looked at the ceiling. Part of it seemed to be the underside of steps leading up. On the side near the kitchen door, the ceiling was only a foot above the floor. Where Kate stood, the ceiling reached above her head. On the far end, it evened out at the height of the second floor. Even a tall man could stand there.

"Well, that explains one mystery!" exclaimed Josie, still holding her kitten out of Lutfisk's reach. "At least we know where Calico's been hiding."

"But there's something we *don't* know," answered Kate. "Where's your papa's ring? And the buckle for my ski?"

Once more Kate held out the candle and gazed up and down the walls. The room seemed empty.

The others looked just as disappointed as Kate felt. It'd be fun having a secret place. There were all kinds of ways they could use it. Yet they hadn't solved the mystery of the missing ring.

Erik felt around the sides of the small room, pressing here and there for a secret panel. Anders checked the wooden floor. Josie held Calico away from the dog. Finally Josie and Erik gave up and left the little room.

Then Kate noticed Lutfisk. After sniffing his way around, he stopped near the entrance. Dropping to his belly, the dog rested his head on his paws.

As Anders left the room, he called Lutfisk. "Here, boy!" But the dog refused to move.

"Lutfisk!" Anders ordered again.

The dog yipped, wiggled forward a few inches on his belly, then stopped.

Still inside the secret room, Kate waited for Lutfisk to obey. "What's the matter with him?"

Anders slapped his leg. "C'mon, boy. You can't get by with that."

Lutfisk snuffled his nose closer to the wall.

Puzzled, Kate kneeled down on the floor next to the dog. Then she saw what she'd missed before. Something bright. Something almost hidden in the darkness. In a crack near the door there was something shiny. The dog's nose pointed right to it!

Tugging Lutfisk's collar, Kate pulled him back just a bit. Sure enough, she was right!

Setting the candle holder on the floor, Kate reached forward and slid her fingers into the narrow crack. Out came a small round object.

"Papa's ring!" shrieked Josie. In the light of the candle the diamonds and rubies sparkled.

Anders grinned at Kate. "Pretty good for a dog, huh?"

Kate grinned back and dug deeper. Next she found the buckle for her ski. Clutching the buckle and ring, she put them on the low table near the shelves.

Josie's eyes glowed. "We can pay for the farm!"

"Just in time!" exclaimed Kate. Relief washed over her like a giant wave. "Tomorrow your father can go to Minneapolis."

"I'll go find him," said Josie, and started for the door. She almost crashed into her mother.

When Mrs. Swenson heard the news, she threw up her hands and rushed out, "Henry! Henry! We can make the payment in time!"

Soon she returned with Mr. Swenson. As Josie told him everything, her father's expression changed from shock, to relief, to joy. Twice he tried to ask questions and could not. Quiet tears wet his roughened cheeks. When at last he could speak, he simply said, "Thanks be to God!"

Erik and Anders showed Mr. Swenson the secret room, then closed the door. In the shadow beneath the bottom shelf, the hole once more disappeared.

"All someone had to do was slide the ring through," Erik

explained. "It lodged in the crack behind."

"This used to be a one-room log house," Mr. Swenson told them. "The people before us added the kitchen. Maybe that's when they made the secret room."

In spite of the celebration, Kate felt uneasy. "We still don't know who did it," she said. "Who pushed the buckle and ring through the hole? And who took the ring out again?"

A moment later, Kate answered her own question. "It can't be Maybelle. She'd never hide the ring here."

"That leaves Stretch," said Anders.

"Nay," said Mr. Swenson, and his wife nodded agreement. "It's not Stretch. But whoever it is had to be able to reach the ring. I hid it high on those shelves."

Then Kate remembered something. "We still have a clue we haven't figured out. The smudges on those boxes. If they're small fingerprints, who made them?"

In that moment Kate noticed the quiet. No longer was Stretch splitting wood outside the window.

Josie jumped up. "Uh-oh! I forgot I'm supposed to watch Becca. Where is she?" Running out, Josie found the three-year-old in the kitchen.

Following Josie into the large room, Becca walked over to the low table. She pointed to the buckle. "Pretty," she said. Then she picked up the ring. "Pretty," she said again.

"That's right," agreed Josie. "It's pretty. Put it back on the table."

But Kate was noticing Becca's fingers. *Small. Small enough for the prints on the boxes? Could it be?*

In that moment Becca held up the ring. The fading sunlight caught the gold, diamonds, and rubies.

"Pretty." Becca closed her chubby fist around the ring and carried it over to the shelves. Dropping to her knees, Becca reached under the bottom shelf and pushed the ring through the hole.

"Did you see *that*?" asked Kate.

Josie had already reached the three-year-old. "Did you do that before?" Josie asked.

Slowly Becca nodded. Her bottom lip quivered.

"I can't believe it!" Josie exclaimed. "All the times we looked for that ring!"

Becca stared at Josie, her eyes bright with tears.

"And you took it, Becca?"

Ducking her head, Becca let out a long wail. She reached out for her mother.

Mrs. Swenson took the little girl in her arms. "Josie's right," she said to Becca. "You mustn't take things that don't belong to you." Mrs. Swenson started toward the kitchen. "Mama needs to have a talk with you. Yah, sure."

As she reached the door, Mrs. Swenson turned back. "Where was Stretch going so fast? I saw him running toward the woods. I called, but he didn't come back."

Erik looked at Anders. "He heard you, Anders." Erik's voice sounded tight with anger.

"He heard you and ran," said Kate. "Ran away!"

"Stretch was here," said Becca in a small voice. "He here when you mad."

Anders stared at the little girl as though suddenly realizing what he'd done.

"Mr. Swenson asked us to help Stretch," Erik went on. "We helped him all right! We accused him of something he didn't do. We helped him give up!"

Anders wiped his hand across his face as though trying to push away what he saw.

Shadows, thought Kate as she glimpsed the pain in her brother's eyes. *Anders accusing Stretch for something he didn't do.*

"I was wrong," said Anders, his voice low and ashamed.

Watching him, Kate wondered about something. *Have I done the same thing with Maybelle? From the moment I met Maybelle, I didn't trust her. Was that wrong? Or am I uneasy for a reason?*

Now Anders struggled to his feet. "What can I do? I've got to tell Stretch I'm sorry."

"Let's all look for him," answered Kate. With all her heart she wanted to make things right for Stretch.

Erik grabbed his coat. "We've got to find him now!"

Kate agreed. "Before he's gone for good!"

"I'll go," said Mr. Swenson. "I'll hitch up the horses."

"If you take the road, we'll look on the paths where you can't drive," said Erik. "Sounds as if Stretch started through the woods."

"You can't run on that ankle," Mrs. Swenson warned Anders as all of them pulled on their coats.

"Kate can't go alone," Anders told her. "It'll soon be dark. She's afraid of the woods at night."

For once Kate didn't argue with him. Though she'd never admitted it to Anders, it was true.

"I'll go as far as I can," said Anders, pulling Papa's old work boots over his woolen socks. "We'll stick together."

As they went out, the winter sun was low in the sky. Long shadows stretched away from the trees and bushes. Erik took the lead, heading into the woods on the path where Mrs. Swenson saw Stretch disappear. Anders followed, with Kate and Josie close behind.

Soon Erik pointed down to footsteps in the snow. "That's him!"

For a time it was easy to follow the tracks. Not many people had come this way. But the boot prints were far apart, as if Stretch were running. Was there any hope of catching him?

To Kate's surprise Anders kept up. As they reached a fork in the trail, Erik stopped. He and Anders studied the snow.

They had come through the woods on a less traveled path. Now they needed to veer left or right. On both of those wider trails the snow was beaten down, crisscrossed by people, horses, and sleighs. An icy crust had formed around many of the prints.

Erik walked six or seven yards in one direction, looking at the snow. Coming back, he tried the other trail. Finally he shook his head. "Too many people."

"We need to split up," said Kate. "Take *both* ways."

Erik nodded. "But you and I are the only ones Stretch will trust, even a little. So one of us better go each way. Maybe he'll talk to us."

Anders looked at Kate. "Let's take the trail to our house. If Stretch goes to his family's farm, he'll head that way."

Erik agreed. "And Josie and I will take the other direction.

There's an old log cabin down that path. If Stretch knows about it, he might head there."

As they started off, Anders set the pace. His long legs stretched out, and Kate had to run to keep up.

"We've got to hurry," Anders called to her. "Stretch had a good head start."

Kate tried to move faster. The path was uneven with boot prints edged with ice.

Farther on, Anders turned back again. "He'll get away for good!" But a moment later, Anders cried out.

As Kate rounded a bend, she found him rolling on the ground.

"Ow, ow, ow!" he moaned, clutching his ankle. "I stepped on it wrong."

Catching up, Kate kneeled down beside him. She felt scared all the way through. How would Anders get home? And how could they ever catch Stretch?

"What should I do?" she asked.

"It feels like I got stabbed." Anders spoke between clenched teeth.

A tight knot formed in Kate's stomach. For a long moment she stared at her brother, feeling helpless. "If only we had one of those newfangled telephones!" she said.

Anders hooted. "Lot of good that'd do out here in the woods."

"I could call and get help. I could call Stretch's farm and see if he's there."

"Kate, talk sense!" Anders said sharply. "You have to keep going."

"Go on?" Kate looked around. The woods seemed eerie in the half-light that lingered before the sun slipped over the horizon.

"You don't have any choice."

"Go all by myself?" Kate stared at the underbrush. Here and there dead brown leaves fluttered in the wind. What animals lurked behind the brush where she couldn't see? "It'll be dark soon," she said.

"Stretch will get away," Anders told her. "He'll leave the area, and we'll never see him again. You're the one who told me how awful that would be!"

Once more Kate gazed at the woods and the long, dark shadows. Her dread of those shadows rushed up, real and frightening. When she spoke again, her voice trembled. "I can't do it, Anders." She stumbled over the words.

22

The Dangerous Chase

*Y*ou have to," Anders said firmly. "You have to keep going."

"I can't," said Kate, staring at the darkening woods. "I can't do it alone."

Anders sighed. "You'll be all right. The bogeyman won't get you."

"The bogeyman?" Kate's heart leaped into her throat again. She'd been wondering about the wild animals.

"Well, what is it you're scared of? Stop thinking about yourself."

"I'm not just thinking about myself!"

"Aren't you, scaredy-cat?" His voice goaded Kate, making her more angry than scared.

But then she wondered about Anders. "What will happen to you?"

"I'll make it somehow. Just help me up."

As Kate grasped his arm, Anders struggled to his good foot. "Get me a stick," he said.

When Kate found a stout branch along the path, he told her, "Now get going. You have to catch Stretch."

With one last look at Anders, Kate started off, half running, half walking. The snow on the path was still pitted with prints of all kinds. Wherever the woods opened to the sun, those prints were stiff with ice. The uneven edges made it hard going.

Once Kate looked back. The trees and undergrowth hid Anders from view.

In that instant a bird whirred up in front of her. Kate jerked to a halt, shuddering with surprise. Just an old grouse, she knew. But telling herself that didn't stop her trembling.

All around her, the woods seemed alive. Somewhere behind Kate, something rustled. Then she heard another sound—a scruffy, scuffling sound.

A bear? A bear in the woods?

Kate fled, running until she could no longer breathe and had to slow down. *Sarah Livingston told me there'd be bears.* It made no difference that her friend Sarah lived in Minneapolis, and Kate lived here. Sarah knew.

As Kate caught her breath, she heard the sound again. As though an animal walked on the snow's icy crust. Coming closer and closer.

Filled with panic, Kate turned in the direction of the sound. A short distance away a squirrel scampered across the snow.

Kate felt foolish. Then she remembered. *Bears hibernate in winter. They're sleeping now.*

The woods silent around her, Kate stood there. But she couldn't push away her fear. Again she started out, walking as fast as she could. Soon the sun would edge over the horizon. Soon it would be dark.

She'd come to know the woods during the day. Sometimes the woods even seemed a friend. But at night the animals came out. Were they peering at her with their little beady eyes?

I'm alone, Kate told herself. *What's behind that bush—the one right near the trail?*

I'm all alone in these awful woods. Kate's steps slowed. *But am I?*

"Stop thinking about yourself," Anders had said. Kate knew he was right. She felt ashamed.

Shadows. Some are real. Some I imagine. But there's a real shadow in Stretch's life. Being accused of something he didn't do.

Then Kate remembered Mama's verse: "Casting all your care upon him, for he careth for you." As Kate broke into a run, she started to pray. "Jesus, you cared so much. You even died on the cross. You did something really hard for me. Will you help me do something hard for Stretch?"

Once, far ahead, Kate thought she saw the tall thin boy. Was it Stretch? She called out his name, but no answer came. Then a cramp in her side forced her to a walk.

As Kate reached the top of the hill near the farmhouse, the red-orange sun slipped behind the trees. In the fading light Kate looked across the yard toward the granary and barn. "The sheep!" Kate muttered to herself. "They're still outside!"

As she started toward the pasture, long shadows darkened the sides of buildings. Spying a tall thin shadow along the granary, Kate stopped.

What was it? A tree?

The shadow did not move.

I imagined something, Kate told herself, and hurried on.

As she neared the barn, more shadows darkened the log wall. Kate shivered, remembering the night one of those shadows moved.

Swallowing her fear, she forced herself on. As she drew closer to the barn, a darker shadow separated from the rest. A slender shadow, not much taller than Kate.

The shadow slid sideways, across the log wall. Then it slipped around the corner of the barn closest to the wagon track.

Did I imagine it? For a split second Kate stood there, wondering. She remembered the times Anders and Erik had warned her: "Don't jump into something you can't handle."

Then Kate knew. She hadn't imagined it!

She also felt sure of something else. *I know who the shadow is!*

In that instant, everything fell into place. Starting to run, Kate headed for the end of the barn farthest from the wagon track. Lifting the top rail, she climbed through the fence on that side.

Replacing the pine rail, she ran across the barnyard to the fence on the other side. Once more, she lifted the top rail and slipped through. Reaching the far pasture, she looked around.

On the other end of the barn, near the wagon track, a dark shape pressed close to the wall. Face turned away, back toward Kate, the person leaned out, peering around the far corner.

Kate crept forward slowly, quietly. Just before she reached the end of the barn, the person turned.

"Hi, Maybelle," Kate said quietly, feeling she had known all along.

A surprised look crossed the other girl's face.

Then Kate saw Maybelle's coat. Older than the one she usually wore, this coat had black buttons. Even in the fading light Kate saw a button missing.

"I thought so!" exclaimed Kate. "You're the one who took Wildfire from the barn. You've been riding her at night! Why? Just because you wanted your own way?"

Maybelle's look of surprise faded. She smiled. "I don't know what you're talking about, Kate," she said in the sweet voice Kate had learned not to trust.

"Yes, you do," Kate answered. "You know exactly what I'm talking about. And you're going to talk to Anders!"

"Anders?" Maybelle tossed her head, and her long thick hair swung about her shoulders. "If it comes to that, Anders will believe *me*, not you!"

"It'll come to that," Kate growled. "And he's my brother. He'll believe me!" Reaching deep into her coat pocket, Kate felt the button she'd found.

Maybelle sniffed. Her lips parted, as if to answer. But then she glanced beyond Kate.

"Look!" she exclaimed.

Unwilling to be tricked, Kate refused to turn. She knew that only pasture lay behind her. A pasture surrounded by a fence that enclosed the sheep.

"You can't fool me!" she told Maybelle.

But Maybelle hushed her. "I'm not trying!" For once her voice sounded sharp.

Then Kate saw the fear in the other girl's eyes. "What's the matter?" Kate whispered.

"See along the fence?" asked Maybelle.

Kate whirled, facing the pasture Papa Nordstrom had been

clearing. Tree stumps rose from the snow, dotting the field. Along the far side, the woods grew close to the fence line.

There the sheep huddled, backs to the north wind. Heads down, they grazed on the long dead grass growing up around the stumps.

Just beyond the stumps crept a shadow. A shadow that moved toward the sheep. In the dusk that shadow looked like a large gray dog.

"Lutfisk?" Kate whispered, so afraid she could barely speak. But in the next instant she remembered how Anders trusted his dog with the sheep.

Then Kate knew. "It's a wolf."

Kate had never seen one, yet she knew.

23

Northern Lights

$\mathcal{T}$he fear clutching Kate's stomach moved into her throat. Her knees felt weak, as though she couldn't move.

Along the far side of the field, the gray shadow stopped and lifted its head. Then it moved on, once more creeping toward the sheep.

Kate knew she had no choice. In that moment her legs seemed to work. She ran forward and grabbed a loose rail from the top of the fence. Picking it up, she started toward the wolf.

The wolf paused, looked her way.

Kate froze. *What if he comes after me?*

Beyond the wolf, Kate saw something move. Another shadow? More wolves? Kate's breath caught in her throat.

Then one of the sheep bleated. *Baaaa!*

Two other sheep looked up. Kate glanced their way. They still huddled near the fence, clustering together, helpless.

From behind them came another movement.

In that instant Kate felt certain. Two more wolves, maybe three?

Kate's hands tightened on the rail. Step by step she started forward, holding the rail in front of her.

Once more the nearest wolf raised his head. He sniffed, as though catching her scent, and waited. Again Kate's knees felt weak. As she held the rail, her hands trembled.

Then Kate heard quick steps from behind. Someone grabbed the rail from her hands.

Whirling, Kate saw his face. "Stretch!"

The tall boy charged, holding the rail ahead of him.

The wolf closest to the sheep stopped, waited.

Stretch's long legs carried him across the snowy field.

Suddenly the nearest wolf dropped back, slinking away. The other wolves followed. Their gray bodies melted into the darker shadows of the woods.

Kate breathed deeply. She wanted to cry. Then she wanted to laugh. *All this time I've been afraid*, she thought. *Afraid of shadows. Afraid of howls. And the wolves are afraid of US!*

Stretch stayed between the woods and the sheep. Using the rail to guide them, he started the animals back toward Kate.

"You're *here*!" she cried, still feeling she couldn't think. "I was afraid I couldn't catch you."

"You wouldn't have," said Stretch. "I saw Maybelle heading toward your barn. I knew she was the one you're lookin' for. I thought, 'Anders he don't trust me. Why should I care about his horse?' "

"But you came back," said Kate. "Why?"

" 'Cause I knew you'd get the blame."

For a moment Stretch was silent, and Kate thought that was all. But when the tall boy spoke again, his voice was low, as if afraid to tell her.

"Remember the birthday party for Anders?" he asked.

Kate remembered, all right. She also remembered thinking that what she did would be important to Stretch.

"I ain't never seen anyone as mean as Maybelle," he said. "But you weren't mean to her. You acted as if it didn't matter."

"So you came back?" Again Kate felt like crying. "Thanks, Stretch." She wished she knew how to say more.

But then she saw his eyes, and knew she didn't have to. Stretch straightened his shoulders and walked tall.

As they neared the barn, Maybelle started to leave. Kate

broke into a run, circling around to cut her off. Maybelle changed directions, heading toward the rail fence back of the barn. She started to crawl through, then stopped.

Looking beyond Maybelle, Kate saw the path from the farmhouse. Erik ran their way. Not far behind came Anders, one arm around Josie's shoulder, his other hand on the stick Kate had given him. He hopped on one foot.

Erik seemed to know what had happened. Leaping into the pasture, he helped Stretch bring in the sheep. Kate kept Maybelle cornered between herself and Anders.

"I caught her here," Kate said when Anders came up. "She's the one who took Wildfire from the barn."

Maybelle smiled at Anders. "You don't really believe I'd do something like that, do you?"

Anders looked from one girl to the other.

"Maybelle's been riding Wildfire," said Kate.

"Anders, you know she's just talking. Kate makes things up."

"No, she doesn't," said Anders. His voice was quiet, but there was no mistaking the sound of it. "Kate isn't just talking. I believe her."

"It's her word against mine!" Maybelle's voice was no longer sweet.

Anders grinned. "I can trust Kate. She's my sister."

In that moment all of Kate's hurt fell away. Inside, she felt as if she were singing.

"You can't prove a thing," challenged Maybelle.

"I want to show you something," said Kate. Reaching deep inside her coat pocket, she found the button. Slowly she pulled it out.

Maybelle stared, but did not reach out for the button. As she looked toward Anders, she lifted her chin. "I was sure you wouldn't mind if I took Wildfire for a ride."

"I'm sure that I *would*!" Anders snapped. "And you better make sure it never happens again!"

As Maybelle slipped off into the shadows, Stretch and Erik brought the sheep close to the barn. Facing Anders, Stretch pulled himself even taller than usual. He seemed to grow two inches.

Anders spoke before Stretch could. "Thanks for saving our sheep," he said.

Kate had seldom heard her brother so humble.

Anders reached out his hand. "I'm sorry, Stretch. I'm sorry for the way I treated you."

Anger flashed across the older boy's face. Lifting his head, Stretch looked proud. For a moment he seemed to debate with himself. Then slowly, without words, he extended his hand.

Looking straight into each other's eyes, Anders and Stretch shook hands.

It was Josie who broke the tension. "Our farm is safe. Your sheep are all right. And Wildfire will be!" Relief filled Josie's laugh. "But I suppose there'll be another mystery."

"I suppose." Anders grinned at Kate. "Before Papa gets home, do you think?"

"I don't know," she answered. "What else can happen around here?" She looked at Erik.

"Plenty!" he exclaimed. "Until you moved here, we never had one mystery to solve!"

A moment later Mr. Swenson drew up with his horses. As he looked toward Stretch and Anders, a relieved smile came to his face. Giving a wave, he headed for home.

The rest of them went to the Windy Hill farmhouse and sat down to Mama's warm supper.

Later, when Josie, Erik, and Stretch started for home, they came back. "Come outside," Erik told Kate and Anders. "We want to show you something."

Together they walked to the edge of the steep hill. There they could see far around. Erik pointed up.

Kate's gaze followed his hand. In the northern sky, long white shafts of light stretched from the horizon upward. The light pulsed through the darkness, seeming to move and grow.

Kate stood there, filled with wonder. "What is it?" she asked.

"Northern lights," replied Erik softly, and even Anders was quiet.

For a time they watched the glowing beams. Gradually the color changed to pale pink, then blue and light green.

As they started back to the house, Anders, Josie, and Stretch walked ahead, talking. Erik and Kate fell behind.

When Kate looked up, she felt surprised to see Erik watching her.

"Happy birthday, Kate," he said.

"Thanks," she answered, feeling strange. So much had happened since the party, she'd forgotten about her birthday.

But Erik was still watching her. "You're different, Kate," he said, his voice low.

"Different?" She drew back, wondering what he meant. "Awful?" She felt afraid to ask.

"Different from other girls. Better." For a long moment Erik looked at her. "Special. Very special."

Kate smiled, knowing he'd given her one of the nicest presents she could receive.

"Thanks, Erik," she said again. The words weren't half enough, but Erik seemed to understand.

When he and Josie and Stretch started for home once more, Kate and Anders turned toward the Windy Hill farmhouse.

As Kate pushed open the door, the warmth and light of the kitchen reached out, seeming to welcome them. The shadows disappeared, melting away into the night, where they belonged.

Acknowledgments

Often I'm asked, "Lois, where do you get the ideas for your novels?"

I've discovered that ideas are everywhere. Yet I need to recognize which ones are good, which are unimportant, and which will help me shape the story I want to tell.

Countless people—more than I can possibly name—have added to my storehouse of ideas. Among these are the following individuals who gave long hours and detailed information: Shirley Anderson, Goodwin Branstad, Myrtle Carlson, Alwin and Imogene Christopherson, Maurice and Arleth Erickson, Edith Falat, Sarah Harmon, Robert and Jean Hinrichs, Herman and Alma Johnson, Gary and Jane Kaefer, Randy and Renee Klawitter, Henry Peterson, Ida Peterson, Roy and Grace Soderbeck, and Helen Tyberg.

Again I'm grateful to Mildred Hedlund for her help with Big Gust, to Eunice Kanne for her book *Big Gust: Grantsburg's Legendary Giant,* and to all the librarians at the public library in Grantsburg, Wisconsin.

Walter and Ella Johnson and Diane Brask offered their knowledge and love of northwest Wisconsin, as well as their time. My parents, Alvar and Lydia Walfrid, continue to answer my never-ending questions.

Jerry Foley, Penelope Stokes, and Terry White gave valuable

assistance with the manuscript. Charette Barta, Ron Klug, and the entire Bethany team provided editorial wisdom, support, and love.

Many individuals—Betty Coleman, Elaine Roub, and more than I can even guess—have helped in quiet and unseen ways. May their caring for me and you as readers be returned to them many times over.

From the time I begin thinking about a book through its early and final drafts, my husband and I talk about ideas. From his rich experience Roy offers suggestions, encouragement, and practical ways of saying, "Keep on in this work that you love." To him I once more give my heartfelt gratitude.

And finally, special thanks to Daniel Johnson, who reminds all of us that "God cares for *you!*"